The Killer

The mind of a killer is an empty thing.

The strings of a puppet are filled with mischief.

Imagine a mind, then, that when a string is pulled somebody will die—an innocent asleep in her bed. Imagine and then quickly forget, lest the impulse pluck deep and make you realize that we are all puppets in a show without rules.

But maybe that is not true.

It doesn't matter. It seems true.

Dusty Shame did not play by any rules. He had killed twice in his life and he was going to kill again. But he didn't enjoy taking human life. He wasn't a psychopath in the traditional sense of the word. He did not dream of blood and screams and feel cold sweat break out over his limbs and experience a rush of sexual satisfaction. He didn't even dislike most people, never mind hate them. No one had ever done anything particularly wrong to him and, until he started to kill, he had never thought of hurting anyone.

Yet tonight would be murder number three.

Three—the one that was supposed to charm.

But where was the charm for poor Dusty?

Where was the reason?

Books by Christopher Pike

BURY ME DEEP
CHAIN LETTER 2: THE ANCIENT EVIL
DIE SOFTLY
THE ETERNAL ENEMY
FALL INTO DARKNESS
FINAL FRIENDS #1: THE PARTY
FINAL FRIENDS #2: THE DANCE
FINAL FRIENDS #3: THE GRADUATION
GIMME A KISS
THE IMMORTAL
LAST ACT
MASTER OF MURDER
MONSTER
REMEMBER ME
ROAD TO NOWHERE
SCAVENGER HUNT
SEE YOU LATER
SPELLBOUND
WHISPER OF DEATH
THE WICKED HEART
WITCH

Available from ARCHWAY Paperbacks

AN ARCHWAY PAPERBACK
Published by POCKET BOOKS
New York London Toronto Sydney Tokyo Singapore

This book is a work of fiction. Names, characters, places and incidents are either products of the author's imagination or are used fictitiously. Any resemblance to actual events or locales or persons, living or dead, is entirely coincidental.

AN ARCHWAY PAPERBACK *Original*

An Archway Paperback published by
POCKET BOOKS, a division of Simon & Schuster Inc.
1230 Avenue of the Americas, New York, NY 10020

ISBN: 0-671-74511-5

First Archway Paperback printing November 1993

10 9 8 7 6 5 4 3 2 1

Cover art by Dru Blair

Printed in the U.S.A.

IL 14 +

For myself.
This dark story written during
those dark nights.

The Wicked Heart

1

The mind of a killer is an empty thing.

The strings of a puppet are filled with mischief.

Imagine a mind, then, that when a string is pulled somebody will die—an innocent asleep in her bed. Imagine and then quickly forget, lest the impulse pluck deep and make you realize that we are all puppets in a show without rules.

But maybe that is not true.

It doesn't matter. It seems true.

Dusty Shame did not play by any rules. He had killed twice in his life and he was going to kill again. But he didn't enjoy taking human life. He wasn't a psychopath in the traditional sense of the word. He did not dream of blood and screams and feel cold sweat break out over his limbs and experience a rush of sexual satisfaction. He didn't even dislike most people, never mind hate them. No one had ever done anything particularly wrong to him, and until he started to kill, he had never thought of hurting anyone.

Yet tonight would be murder number three.

Three—the one that was supposed to charm.

But where was the charm for poor Dusty?

Where was the reason?

The answer was so simple it couldn't be the final answer. Yet it must be put down. Dusty killed so he could rest. It was only when he forever closed the eyes of another that he could close his own eyes and sleep without the dreams and the voice telling him it was time to awaken and continue with the pain.

Of course, such a reason must have meant Dusty was crazy. People who heard voices were invariably insane, experts would say. But few experts had ever been inside a mind the equal of Dusty's. Had they entered, they would have realized that insanity was as mysterious as reason, and that the two were often difficult to separate.

Dusty may have been crazy, but he was also a nice young man.

He was eighteen years old, a senior in high school, six weeks shy of graduation. His grade point average was three point six, and he was taking chemistry, calculus, computer science, and German. He was on his way to college, that is if he didn't make a quick stop at the electric chair first.

He was a handsome young man. His hair was light brown, soft and fine like that of an angel, his eyes green as grass in evening twilight. He was five ten, fit and muscular, but plagued by repeated heartburn. He had a tendency, when in social situations, to be jerky in his movements. But when he was alone, especially when he killed, he moved smoothly and gracefully as a dancer. Always, though, he was quiet. Had he been more talkative, he certainly could have had plenty of dates. And maybe if he had spoken to more girls and listened to their voices instead of the one his head, he wouldn't have become a murderer.

Maybe, maybe not.

Dusty's first two victims had been girls.

It was late Monday night. Dusty drove through the dark California streets of his hometown, Chino—a suburb in San Bernadino County, which adjoined both Los Angeles and Orange counties. He was headed toward his next victim's house. Years ago Chino had been a place to tie a horse in the backyard, but now there were housing developments everywhere. The town had been home for Dusty all his life. He couldn't say he liked the place, though, but that may have been because his had been a sad life.

His next victim was Nancy Bardella and she lived only two miles from him. He knew Nancy from school, unlike the other two he had killed, whom he knew only via the modem lines of a national computer network—*Einstein.* Nancy was in his chemistry lab and class—she sat two rows in front of him, on the right, in class. He had spoken to her a few times, although never at length. She was a pretty girl with long brown hair and dimples that showed when she laughed, which she did often.

Dusty knew from eavesdropping on her conversations that her parents were away for a few days. He had chosen to kill her, instead of another girl, largely because of this fact. Also, Nancy was a sweet girl and seldom had an unkind word to say about anybody. It was important to Dusty that each of his victims be as innocent as possible. In reality, Dusty liked Nancy.

The late April night was warm—the month of May and another southern California summer were around the corner—and the streets all but deserted. Dusty liked the late-night hours best, when the hum of the city was at its gentlest. He was particularly sensitive to crowds and crowd noise; it was as if the mental static of many minds wore on the delicate centers of his brain. Often, just visiting a mall exhausted him. When he did sleep, which he seldom did, it was usually in the daytime, after school.

But he knew tonight, what was left of it, he would sleep well, if he could just kill Nancy and get rid of her body without being caught. Dusty may have loathed what he did, but he didn't want to go to jail. He felt if they locked him up, the voice would go on tormenting him endlessly, and he wouldn't be able to do anything to silence it. That was his greatest fear, although he had others.

Nancy lived at the end of a cul-de-sac in one of

Chino's new housing tracts. Dusty pulled onto her street and cut the engine, allowing the car to coast into Nancy's empty driveway. He disliked bringing his car so close, but it was necessary when it came time to carry the body out. He never left a body behind, the voice was strict about that, and for that reason the parents of his first two victims were still looking for their daughters. He occasionally saw posters advertising rewards for information about their disappearances. He knew that the parents would be searching for their children for a long time.

Nancy had lived in southern California all her life. Dusty knew that her father worked as an engineer at Hughes Aircraft, and that her mother took care of preschoolers. Nancy was an only child. Her best friend was Sheila Hardholt, who was Dusty's lab partner in chemistry. Dusty liked Sheila as well.

The cul-de-sac was well lit, which bothered him. All the new housing tracts in Chino were loaded with lights. The house was also visible from many surrounding houses. If someone were to peek through a window as he was carrying out the body, he would be in serious trouble. But he knew *his* window of vulnerability was brief—maybe a minute at best, only the actual time when he had the body in his hands. If a neighbor were to see him now, sitting in his car, it was doubtful he would sound an alarm. It would be hard to trace his car just from a glance. Red Ford Escorts were a dime a dozen in the L.A. basin. Plus he had smeared his license plate with mud.

Dusty sat in his car a moment, studying the house. There were two stories—Nancy's bedroom was probably on the second. Although most of the houses in the neighborhood had yet to have yards installed, Nancy's parents had spent big bucks on landscaping. The lawn was made up of thick fescu grass, common to the area. Recently planted shrubs hugged the clean orange stucco walls. More important than these details were the six-foot-high walls and the accompanying gates, which would surely be locked. More than likely, he would have to take the body out the front door, something he had not done before.

The walls presented no problem for him. He could climb over them. Sitting in the car, he decided to do just that and then try to find an open window in the back. In his pocket he carried a lock-pick kit. But he had not grown up playing with locks, and his skill at outwitting dead bolt locks was minimal at best. He also had duct tape in his pocket, and knew he could tape a window and break it without making much noise. He did that the night he had visited Stacy Domino's house, the first time he had killed.

His other tools were few: a ball peen hammer, two large heavy-duty green garbage bags, and a white towel. He used the hammer to kill; the narrow head of the ball peen hammer was a more lethal weapon than a regular hammer. The bags were for the body—one for the top half, the other for the bottom. The towel was his special piece of paraphernalia. Just before striking the death blow, usually to the delicate temple area at the side of the skull, he would throw the towel over the girl's head. He made every effort to keep any blood from spilling, leaving the police and the parents with the idea—the *possibility* at least—that their daughter had merely run away or been kidnapped. But neither police nor parents would entertain the latter idea long because no ransom note would be forthcoming.

Yet these possibilities were important to satisfy the voice. They greatly heightened the torment of his acts.

On his hands he wore leather gloves. Always.

Dusty picked up the hammer, the garbage bags, and the towel, and stuffed them into a knapsack that fit over his shoulder. After turning off the overhead light, he silently opened the car door and stepped onto the concrete driveway. He closed the door, but did not shut it completely. He preferred, when he was done, to place the body in the trunk, but if he felt rushed he could set it in the passenger seat. The seats, like the trunk, were covered with clear plastic he had obtained from a garbage bin behind a cleaners. He went to great lengths to prevent staining his car with blood.

He approached the house on the right side, opposite the porch walkway, and was over the brick wall in a moment. The backyard did not please him. Two other houses, elevated slightly above Nancy's, had unobstructed views into her yard. He had to pause to reassure himself that it was late, and that the two other houses looked as asleep as empty buildings.

A quick scan of Nancy's back windows showed him one that was half open. The sight brought him a measure of relief, although his muscles remained taunt and his breathing rapid and uneven. In his lock-pick kit was a small screwdriver. He took it out and slipped it under the bottom edge of the window screen, bending the metal slowly upward. The screen popped free. He set it on the ground and gently eased up the window. A moment later he was able to step inside with a long stretch of his legs.

He was in the living room. The furniture, glimpsed in stabs of yellow streetlight, was new, and the faint smell of fresh paint hung in the air. He stood still for several seconds and forced himself to take long deep breaths. His heartbeat was the sound of toppling stones. He had to convince himself that the beating was not reverberating off the walls, echoing up the stairs to Nancy's sleeping ears.

He started up the stairs, not even bothering to check the downstairs rooms. He *knew* Nancy was up there; he could sense her, but not with his ears or eyes. He could feel her life as clearly as he would feel that life pass through him as he brought it to an end. Her soul would pass through him, he knew, with the blow to the brain, and in that instant something inside him would sigh, and he would have peace, if only for a little while. At least it had been that way before.

It was too easy, too perfect. All three of the bedroom doors on the second floor lay open. Nancy's was the small room on the right, her soft rhythmic breathing drifting into the narrow hallway like a child's song floating on a spring breeze. Nancy, awake had always impressed Dusty as a kind person, but in sleep, even before he saw her, she touched him in a way only a saint could. She *was* innocence; he could almost hear the angels singing in her dreams. Strangely, this quality, this goodness, didn't make it harder for him to kill her, but easier. Or maybe it was not so strange because Dusty was in many ways like his nickname, *Dust,* and viewed everything from the ground level, where the insects that crawled through the mud were the best friends of the flowers that scented the air with their perfume.

Dusty moved to the open doorway and stood looking down on Nancy. She lay on her back, dressed in an oversize T-shirt, white panties, a sheet draped loosely over her tan legs. Her brown hair spread across her pillow, so perfect, like fabric woven of silk threads. Her right elbow was cocked at a sharp angle, her right hand pressed to her chin as if she were deep in thought. Her other arm hung over the side of the bed, the hand almost touching the floor, completely unafraid of the bogeyman that might lurk under the box springs. But of course she was not scared, Dusty thought, angels were watching over her.

So was something else.

As old as the angels.

Dusty removed the towel and hammer from his knapsack.

He wanted it to be quick. He didn't want her to suffer. Still, the thought of the blood plagued him, the evidence of the struggle it would leave. He had to get the towel in position without waking her. He had been able to do that with his second victim because she had been an extremely heavy sleeper. He knew that because of her loud snoring. But he did not believe Nancy would be so easy. He considered the possibilities for several seconds before coming up with a plan.

He would alter the point where he usually struck. He would not hit Nancy on the temple, but directly on the forehead. He would toss the towel over her face and strike an instant later. The first blow might not kill her—the skull was thick in front—but it would stun, and there would be time for others. He knew, though, even as he moved closer to the bed, that timing was critical. If he did not kill her quickly, she would scream, and both her bedroom windows were wide open. He did not want her to scream; he did not want her to know that she was about to die.

In his left hand was his towel, in his right the hammer. He stepped within a foot of the bed and felt cold sweat drip down his arms. Yet suddenly he could no longer hear his heartbeat, his breathing even, only the sound of her breathing, her life, her identity. Even though Dusty believed her soul would survive his attack, he did not think her personality would. He believed, in heaven, no soul could remember having been on Earth. He believed that it would be impossible to enjoy true peace with such memories, especially with such memories as he had. Nancy would be Nancy for only a second more.

Dusty tossed the towel onto her face.

It landed smoothly, a tissue drifting over a reclining doll.

Dusty raised his hammer to strike.

Just then Nancy sat up. He would have said she bolted upright; she caught him so completely by surprise. Yet she moved so easily, so without fear, that it seemed as if her own mother had awakened her. The towel fell from her face onto her lap. Her eyes popped open and she looked at him. Her expression wasn't one of fright or surprise, although she was only partially awake. There wasn't a hint of recognition in her expression. Her voice came out like that of a small yawning child.

"Hello," she said.

Dusty struck with his hammer. Because he meant to hit her as she lay flat on her back, his blow landed at an odd angle. The hammer smashed her forehead, between the eyebrows, but the bulk of the force of the blow was directed lower. He ended up crushing the bridge of her nose. He actually heard the faint sound of shattering cartilage. Nancy's head dropped *forward* as she was hit, although, remarkably, her eyes remained open. He could tell by her eyelashes. Blood dripped from her nose onto his towel, her T-shirt. Dusty didn't know if her open eyes signaled consciousness; he doubted it. But he wasn't taking any chances. He raised the hammer again and struck a crushing blow to the top of her skull. This time the sound was loud, as the strong bone splintered beneath the cold steel.

Nancy toppled farther forward.

He caught her as she fell, dropping his hammer to the floor, and quickly wrapped her head in his towel. There was blood, both from her face and the top of her head, but not a great deal. For a moment he held her, held her as if he were giving her an affectionate hug, and it was good. Yes, it was just right. *Something,* a gust of warm air perhaps, a brush of astral matter maybe, left her body, left her lifeless, and touched him as it passed. He felt the familiar sigh of pleasure inside, the relief it brought, the silence—the silence of evil, so close to the silence of God. Dusty thought of God right then and wondered why God made him go to such extremes to find peace. He was grateful that Nancy was at peace. He couldn't imagine her life as being that happy, her frequent laughter aside. He couldn't imagine a happy life for anyone, period.

After a bit, Dusty eased Nancy's body off the bed and onto the floor, careful to keep the towel wrapped firmly around her head. She felt remarkably light, soft, still warm, even through his gloved hands—it really was nice to hold her. He took one of the green garbage bags from his knapsack and, leaving the towel in place, eased the opening over the top of her head, over her chest and back, down to her waist. Only one thing troubled him as he worked and that was his missing her breathing. He had enjoyed listening to it, and it was sad it was over for good.

He reached for the second bag, and when he had her completely covered he took out his duct tape and sealed the bags together. From experience he knew the tape would not break. He had constructed the equivalent of a body bag, and it pleased him to know that Nancy was safe inside.

Now came the hard part, or at least, the dangerous part. He had to get rid of the body, and he had to do so before the sun came up, which would happen in approximately three and a half hours. Tucking his hammer in his knapsack he crossed to her desk and grabbed her purse and stashed it in his bag as well. Taking this one item, he knew, went a long way toward creating the impression that Nancy had run away from home, at least for the police. The parents, of course, would never believe it.

Dusty hastily made the bed and gave the room a quick going over, making sure he had left no evidence of his visit. Then he did something that contradicted all his previous actions, all the care he had taken.

He took a small square card and placed it on top of Nancy's bed.

Where anybody could see it.

A card with a unique symbol on it.

Dusty knelt and carefully lifted the body into his arms. It was *the body* now, nothing more. He started down the stairs.

Before leaving the house, through the front door, Dusty set down his burden and quickly replaced the screen on the window through which he had entered. He shut the window as well. He knew the police would examine each window for signs of forced entry, but he believed they would learn nothing from the screen he had popped out. He had been careful not to dent the metal with his screw-driver.

Dusty peeked out the front door before stepping outside with the body. His luck held; the neighbor-hood continued to slumber. He closed the door with his foot as he left, but did so carefully, making hardly a sound, making sure it was locked. A moment later he was at his car. He had to set the body down on the driveway to get his keys out, the trunk open. He cautioned himself that he was exposed now, under the scrutiny of streetlights, but his confidence rode high. This had happened on the two previous kills. He would start the night as a nervous wreck and then feel invincible once the body was in his hands. At the same time, he knew the trap of being over confident. When he was scared he took every precaution. Fear, he believed, sharpened the mind, it did not dull it.

He set the body onto the clear plastic that lined his trunk, the head making a soft thud as it rolled to the side, a puppet dropping from the end of a string that had been cut. He closed the trunk as soundlessly as he had opened and closed every door and window in the house. Then he climbed into the car and put the key in the ignition.

Starting the car was dangerous. People, if they were awake, often glanced out their windows when a car nearby was started. Turning over the engine would be the loudest noise he had made since entering the cul-de-sac. Fortunately, his car was only a couple of years old and started without prodding. He backed out of the driveway the instant the engine caught. He was out of the cul-de-sac within sixty seconds of leaving the house with the body.

A couple of miles north of Chino ran Interstate 10, a freeway well known to transcontinental travelers. It was possible to ride I-10 from one end of the country to the other. Dusty got on I-10 and headed east toward Interstate 15, another freeway well known to southern California residents—it being the straight road to Las Vegas. Dusty headed north on 15 in the direction of Vegas and passed through a portion of the mountains that hemmed in the L.A. basin. He was careful not to speed, but within forty minutes of leaving Nancy's house, he was in the desert. He drove with the window down, the night air turning warmer the farther he drove, dryer. He left Interstate 15 for a lesser known freeway, 395, and plowed through the dark night, lit occasionally by the glare of his headlights on a tall cactus. Traffic was sparse, mostly long distance truckers, trying to get a headstart on another weary day on the road. Once on 395, he relaxed more and let his speed creep up. It was seldom the police bothered with the road, he knew. He had been on 395 a few times lately. It wasn't far off this desert highway that he buried his victims.

The spot was his alone. He was quite sure no one else knew about his cave, or else, he believed, he would not have been directed there in the first place. He had come upon it a few days before he visited Stacy Domino. He had found it in the middle of the day, when the sun was directly overhead and frying everything; the narrow opening at the end of the gully, the opening, hidden behind a big rock, that led into the cool cave with the fine sand floor. Intuitively, even before he dug and confirmed his feeling, he had known there were other bodies buried there. Parched skeletons with clean skulls that had not lost their grins.

Twenty miles along on 395, at the top of a low rise he knew even in the dark, Dusty suddenly veered off the road and plowed into a landscape that could have been sliced from the far side of the moon. Dust swam around his Escort and he had to use his windshield wipers and wiper fluid. Yet he was still on a road of sorts, although it had been abandoned years ago to the snakes and tumbleweed. There was no house along the dirt path, though, not even a deserted shack and he wondered why it had ever been made. It didn't matter. He was as isolated as he could be in the United States and there was no one on his tail.

It was a tall succulent that was his next marker—a Joshua tree, half dead, with a withered arm bent from the weight of years, bent precisely in the direction of the cave. The voice knew about the Joshua and said it was to be taken as a sign of past triumphs. Seeing it, Dusty veered to the right once more. The car bounced on the rocks and sand, and he could hear the body rolling around in the trunk. He always hosed off his car at a gas station before he returned home.

Approximately two miles off the dirt road he was forced to park before a mound of boulders set in a staggered pattern that allowed no cars to trespass. Physically, the next task was the most grueling of the whole night. The cave was half a mile away, but that was far to carry a body, even one that weighed only a hundred pounds. Then, even before he could dig the grave, he had to retrace his steps and return to the car for the shovel. It was impossible for him to carry the body and the shovel at the same time.

The night air was dry, even for the desert, and after climbing out of the car he wished he had brought a water bottle. He briefly considered carrying the body to the cave and then driving back to the road to find a large Coke before digging the grave. But he checked his watch and knew that was foolish. He had two and a half hours before sunrise and he would need half that time to clean up the night's work. He still wanted to get at least three hours of sleep before school started. It would not do to miss class immediately after a killing.

The moon had already set and the area was as black as the bottom of a dry well. Before lifting the body out of the trunk, he grabbed his flashlight, turned it on, and jammed it in his belt so that the beam shone around his feet. It was not ideal, but he walked slowly while carrying a body, and the light would be enough to keep him from stumbling. With everything in place, he leaned over and picked up the green garbage bags.

Desert temperatures were dangerous to underestimate. It was four in the morning and it had to be in the mid-eighties. Dusty had to stop to catch his breath four times on the way to the cave, and each time he felt as if he would collapse from dehydration. But once he reached the cave, and lowered his head and back, and squirmed around the tall narrow stone that shielded the opening, he felt better. Fully into the cave, he was able to stand completely erect, and here the temperature was twenty degrees lower than outside. He had often wondered at the coolness of the place and suspected there was a subterranean stream under it. When he sat completely still in the cave for a period of time, which he had done after burying his last victim, he heard a faint gurgling sound.

Emitting a deep sigh of relief, Dusty moved to the rear of the cave and set the body down in the fine white sand. He didn't stop to rest. It was best to finish the job, he knew, before he relaxed and his muscles cramped up. He turned and hurried out of the cave and back to his car.

The entire process of digging the grave, setting the body inside, and covering it took over an hour, even working with the soft sand. That was because Dusty never skimped on the depth of the holes; he lay his bodies at least five feet under, always mindful that a wild animal could smell the corpse and dig it up. He never paused after he began to shovel the sand over what was left of Nancy Bardella. By now his mind was remarkably empty.

There was a hint of light in the east when he finally reentered the city of Chino. Before going home he stopped at an automated car wash and deposited his four quarters and soaped and hosed down his car. A Pepsi machine stood in the corner of the lot and he guzzled down four cans of soft drinks. At the car wash he threw away the plastic that had lined his seats and trunk in a large dumpster, noting with a trace of satisfaction that there was not a drop of blood anywhere. Finally he removed his gloves. It was always the last thing he did. He headed for home confident that he had not left a shred of evidence linking him to the crime.

Except for the card. The symbol.

Why did he leave it?

Because the voice said he had to.

But even the card, he thought, did not relate to him.

It simply related the crimes to one another. And to the past.

The voice said it was important.

Dusty lived with his invalid mother and an illegal immigrant from El Salvador who helped take care of his mother. His mom was a fifty-year-old widow, a victim of fate that had snatched away her husband when Dusty was only nine years old, and then taken her mind a few months later. Dusty's mother, though only middle-aged, had Alzheimer's. What was left of her brain did not allow her to feed herself, never mind find the bathroom. Fortunately—if such a word could be used to apply to anything in Dusty's life—Mr. Shame had died with a large life insurance policy. Dusty was spared the need to work full-time, and his mother was able to avoid the questionable care of a state-run home.

His mother was a vegetable. She could not talk, did not even recognize him, and he seriously doubted she remembered her own name. She could still walk, although like an arthritic penguin, if she had someone to lead her. But all she did all day was sit in the living room and stare at the ashes in the fireplace. It was as if those ashes were the last thread that connected her, however tenuously, to the world. She would emit a faint cry if he or the live-in helper started to clean the fireplace. It had been that way since Mr. Shame died.

Dusty loved his mother very much.

Mrs. Hilda Garcia was the woman from El Salvador. From what Dusty could gather, she had six children back home and sent them all but a fraction of her salary. Apparently her husband had been killed in a misunderstanding over the price of a bottle of beer. She was almost as reclusive as his mother, and would sit for long hours in her bedroom watching Spanish programs. Her English was as poor as her cooking. Dusty lived alone with two women with whom he could not really communicate.

Dusty parked on the street in front of his house and entered through the side door. He didn't worry that Mrs. Garcia would take note of his unusual hours and question him. She was a heavy sleeper, and she minded her own business. Sometimes, though, because of the looks she gave him, he wondered if he frightened her. Yet the looks were rare, and basically they got along fine. Dusty never thought of himself as a scary person.

Before retiring for what was left of the night, Dusty stopped in to check on his mother. She slept flat on her back, on top of the bed, with both knees bent up. She had slept that way every night since she had begun to lose her mind. A yellow nightlight glowed in the corner. Her nightgown was long and woolen, too warm for April, and stained from endless accidents with food. From the sound of her breathing he assumed she was asleep, but as he moved closer he saw that her eyes were open. She did not turn her head as he approached. She gave no sign that she knew he was there.

"Mom," he said. "Are you all right?"

He often asked her that question, although she never answered it. Her eyes continued to stare at the ceiling. He sat on the bed beside her and took her hand. Her flesh was as dry as the dust he had poured onto Nancy Bardella's corpse.

"I had a good night," he said. "Things went well. I don't think there'll be any follow-up problems."

On occasion, he also talked to her about the murders he committed, but only in a roundabout way, never coming out and saying he had killed. At those times her breathing would quicken, and he would imagine she understood. He didn't know why he did this.

"I should go to bed now," he said, squeezing her hand. "This is a good time for me to rest, you know, after the job's done." He leaned over and kissed her forehead, and as he did so, her eyes suddenly closed. "Don't worry about me, Mom," he whispered in her ear. "Your boy is doing well. He's doing the best he can."

Dusty went to his room and shut his door. His tools, the hammer and so on, were still in the trunk of his car, where he would leave them until later. He stripped down to his shorts and climbed between the sheets. He closed his eyes for a moment and listened for the voice. It wasn't there and he was relieved. He had to get up in three hours, but he knew he would sleep deeply, and hopefully he would feel good when he awoke. It had been so long since he felt good.

Just before Dusty dozed off, he thought of the way Nancy had looked at him when she had awakened, the instant before he had hit her with the hammer. She had been half asleep, true, and startled, but he realized now that she must have recognized him. He wondered, briefly, if the last image in her life had stayed with her as she crossed over to the other side. But then he reminded himself that angels never remembered the earth once they were in heaven.

It was important he never forget that, he told himself.

2

Sheila Hardholt sat in the back of chemistry lab on Friday with her partner, Dusty Shame, mixing acids and bases in test tubes and trying to figure out how much salt and water they were supposed to get in return. She did these things with only a fraction of her brain. The larger part of her mind dwelt on a problem that had been plaguing her for the last week. It had been seven days since her boyfriend, Matthew Jaye, had told her they were through.

"It was there, Sheila. I wasn't lying to you when I said I loved you. And I still do love you. But—"

Oh, that *but.* It didn't seem right that so much pain could follow such a small word. And it had all started so beautifully.

She had seen Matt around school for two and a half years before they got involved at the end of their junior year. She had always thought he was attractive, especially his long brown hair, which he wore in a ponytail like Steven Seagal's. But she had never shared a class with him or had any reason to talk to him at length. But then, the previous May, she had been in the local library researching a paper she had to write for her history class, something about ancient Greece, when she bumped into him. He was sitting in the back with his feet up on a chair reading an old *Playboy* magazine, a magazine she didn't care for. But he did nothing to hide it from her as she walked by. In fact, he smiled at her and said hi.

"You're Sheila, aren't you?" he asked. "I've seen you around school. My name's Matt."

"Yeah, Matt, I've seen you, too. How's it going?" She nodded to his magazine. "Doing research for anatomy class?"

He didn't blush. "I know it will sound unbelievable, but I didn't take this magazine out to look at the pictures. There's an article in here about searching for buried treasure, which is something I've always wanted to do."

"Uh-huh. I believe you."

"It's true, really."

She decided to take him at his word. He was cute. "Sounds exotic. Are you interested in treasure under the sea, or in buried gold?"

"Both," Matt said. "I like scuba diving and I love backpacking. Last summer I found a cave in the Sierras filled with Indian artifacts. These were from poor Indians, though, and there were no riches." He pointed to the page he was reading. "But the main stuff I'd like to go after is the gold the Spanish stole from the Incas and the Aztecs. A lot of their ships never made it back to Spain, but sunk off the coast of South and Central America. We're talking about tons of gold." He shrugged. "Of course, I'm only dreaming. You need big bucks and years of research to mount such an expedition." He paused and gave her a close look. "Right now I would be happy to find a single jewel in a muddy river."

Something about his expression made her wonder if his remark carried a double meaning. "Are you exploring any local rivers?" she asked casually.

"Yeah. But they're plenty muddy."

"I guess you'll just have to keep looking."

"I suppose. What brings you here?"

"Homework. History. I have a paper to write."

"Who do you have for history?" Matt asked.

"Baker."

Matt chuckled. "That guy's a trip. Did you know he used to be a Hell's Angel in the sixties? I got drunk with him one night and he told me all about it. He met his wife at a rock concert in Woodstock. In fact, he says he's in some movie about it—one of the naked guys with all the tattoos."

Sheila was intrigued, but wondered if he was putting her on. Mr. Baker was her favorite teacher, and looked more like a poet than a Hell's Angel. Then again, the sixties had been a long time ago.

"He could get fired if the administration knew he was drinking with a student," she said.

"He trusts me not to talk about it," Matt said.

"You're talking to me."

"Yeah, but *I* trust you."

"You don't even know me."

"That ain't my fault."

That stopped her. Maybe he was interested in her. She was suddenly interested in him. She liked his chest—along with his hair—it was wide and strong without ugly bulging muscles. He also had a way of watching her that made her feel sexy. She didn't know how he managed it.

She knew she wasn't bad looking, not a potential model or actress by any stretch of the imagination, but on a good day she had been known to turn heads. Her hair was brown, short with bangs, her eyes blue and bright. Her skin was light, she had trouble tanning without burning, but there wasn't a mark on her. She was slight, with nice legs, delicate hands, and a relatively small chest. She had a way of giggling that made her sound like a six-year-old. But at the same time she was often complimented on the smoothness of her voice, the allure of it. A guy friend at school had once told her she could make a fortune recording books.

"What do you want to know?" she asked.

"Oh, nothing." He paused. "What are you doing this Saturday night?"

"I have to work."

"Really? So do I."

"Then why did you ask me out?" she asked.

"I didn't ask you out."

"Oh." God, she felt like a jerk.

"What are you doing this Friday night?"

No, he was the jerk. Still cute, though, look at those eyes. Warm as a puppy's.

"Are you asking me out?" she asked.

"Maybe."

"I want to know before I answer."

Matt was enjoying himself. He had a confident manner. "I have to know if you'll go out with me before I ask," he said.

"You're just going to have to risk it, buddy."

"You should give me odds at least."

"Why should I do that? You've already insulted me."

"I'm sorry."

"It's all right."

He set his magazine down and leaned toward her. "The reason you have to give me odds is I have to work Friday as well."

"Then your odds are lousy."

"But I might be able to get off," he added.

"You tell me definitely that you'll get off and I'll give you definite odds."

"All right, I'll be sick Friday. What are the chances you'll go out with me?"

"Fifty-fifty."

He frowned. "Sheila, I have laid my cards on the table, risked outright rejection, and you only give me fifty-fifty odds. That's not fair."

"You've risked nothing! You haven't asked me out yet!"

"Ah. I see your point." He swallowed. "I've always wanted to get to know you better."

"Why didn't you just walk up to me at school and say hi?"

"'Cause you're always with that guy."

"What guy?"

"The one who dresses like he's on MTV."

"That guy is my brother."

Matt was impressed. "Most juniors girls are too cool to hang out with their brothers."

"Thank you. But he doesn't dress that weird. You know, that's the second time you've insulted me. Your chances are going down. In fact, I think I have to work Friday night."

Matt acted depressed. "OK. Maybe next year."

"I'll have a boyfriend by then." Then she laughed. "Matt, you're as crazy as I am. Why don't you just ask me?"

He didn't hesitate. "Will you marry me?"

"I don't know. How do I know you're not one of those perverts who reads dirty magazines all the time? I can't marry a pervert."

"I don't read them, I just look at the pictures."

"The truth, finally." She paused to let him sweat a little. But he didn't look like he was sweating. She was the one with the pounding heart. "Yes," she said finally.

"You'll go out with me?"

"No, I'll marry you. Yes, I'll go out with you. But you have to take me some place nice."

"How about a movie?" he asked.

"I love movies."

It wasn't that long before she fell in love with

him. In many ways Matt was a fine upstanding young man, one whom mothers the world over would approve of. His GPA ranged in the high threes; he didn't do hard drugs; and he had a good-paying job. On the other hand, his grade point average was high because he took mostly art and music classes; he drank too much beer; and he was a bartender in a strip joint downtown. He got the job by presenting a fake ID, and demonstrating phenomenal mixing skills that he had picked up from an alcoholic uncle.

But none of that mattered. She loved him because she loved him, and it was just a wonderful coincidence that he loved her as well. Soon they were doing everything together: eating, going to movies, studying, going for hikes—boy, did Matt love to hike. Almost every weekend they drove into the mountains and set off on some secluded trail, walking so far she thought her legs would fall off. The incredible thing about their hikes was not the beauty that surrounded them, but the way being with him made the beauty of the forests that much greater. Being with Matt brought fresh light into Sheila's life, light she had never known before.

They even made love a few times, and although they were both nervous, it was precious to Sheila, his holding her, as if she were the only person in the whole world. But maybe he did not share her feelings, she did not know. It was just that the days after they had sex, Matt always seemed preoccupied. She wondered if the intimacy scared him, or worse, that she was lousy in bed. But when she asked, he always laughed and told her she was the best he had ever had. Then he would lapse again into the distance.

As time went on, they made love less, and his spells lasted longer.

So she had seen it coming, in a way, but it took her completely by surprise, too. Both things were true. She had been waiting to be shocked. But her shock had been much greater than her foresight. She had always felt—before he dropped the axe—that whatever their problem, they could work it out. She had overlooked the possibility that he might not want to bother.

The previous week they had been sitting in his bedroom listening to music and reading when they had *the conversation.* She had started it, foolish girl. It had been one of those days where he hadn't been talking much. She asked him what was wrong, and he gave his usual answer.

"Nothing," he said.

"You look preoccupied," she said.

"You tell me that a lot." He paused and turned a page in his novel. "I'm reading."

"What are you reading?"

"You can see the cover," he replied.

"Sorry I asked."

He put his book down. "What's wrong with you?" he asked.

"Nothing. You're the one with the problem."

"And what is my problem, Sheila?"

"I don't know, you won't tell me."

"I don't have a problem."

"Maybe you do and you don't know it." She paused. "Maybe I'm your problem."

He gave the worst possible answer. He didn't answer. But he lowered his eyes so far that he couldn't have been looking at anything in the room. He picked up his book.

"Matt?" she asked.

"It's a book about Martians."

"Am I your problem?"

"No."

"Am I?" she persisted.

"No." He stopped. "Maybe."

She froze. "Jesus," she whispered. They had been together a whole year, she thought. It couldn't end. He set his book down for the second time and stared at her. She stared back, not knowing what to say.

"I suppose we should talk," he said.

She nodded weakly. "Yeah."

"I really like you, Sheila."

His choice of words did not escape her. *Like.* You were supposed to *like* ice cream and dogs, she thought. You were supposed to love your girlfriend.

"I really love you," she said. Then she began to cry and she hated herself for it because it made her feel so pitiful. So did her next question. "Don't you still love me? You said you did."

He leaned forward and put his arms around her. "It was there, Sheila. I wasn't lying to you when I said I loved you. And I still do love you. But it's changed for me. I don't know how to explain it."

She lowered her head and tried to concentrate on her breathing, trying to stop her trembling. It was all happening so fast, she couldn't assimilate it. Her voice came out cracked and broken.

"How has it changed?" she asked.

"It's nothing you've done. You've been great, the best. It's just that I don't know if I want to be in a relationship anymore." He squeezed her tight. "Sheila, I've wanted to tell you this for a while."

Nothing he said was making her feel any better. "You haven't been happy for a long time?" she asked, amazed.

"No, I didn't mean that. What I mean is, I think you'd be better off with someone else is all."

Her eyes widened. "Are you interested in someone else?"

He met her eyes, and there wasn't a trace of a lie in his expression. "I'm not, Sheila. I promise you, I'm not."

"But then I don't understand. We've been happy together. Why do you have to leave?"

"I'm not leaving. I'm not going anywhere. We'll still be friends, good friends. How could we not be friends?"

She couldn't stop crying. Two minutes ago she'd had a boyfriend, now she had a friend. "But there must be a reason why you don't want to be in a relationship?"

"All I can tell you is that I feel that I need more

time alone." He leaned over and kissed her on the cheek. "And that I'm sorry, very sorry, to have to hurt you like this."

So was she.

That had been a week ago.

They hadn't talked since. Some friends.

She had seen him at school every day. Oh, yes. Seen him talking with his friends, as if his definition of being alone was different from most people. Yet she hadn't seen him talking to any girls and for that she was grateful.

But back to the present moment.

Back to the pain that hadn't lessened.

"We're not going to finish our experiment before class is over," Dusty said.

She realized she had been staring into space for a while. "Do you care?" she asked.

"No," Dusty said. He gestured to the set of six test tubes arranged before them that gave off the foul acidic odor that seemed to have found its way up inside their nasal passages. "I can only mix baking soda and vinegar together so many times."

"I'm wrecking your grade on this experiment," she said.

"I told you, I don't care."

"You're just being a nice guy." Sheila enjoyed working with Dusty for that very reason; he was totally undemanding, although a bit on the nervous side. Before she had fallen madly in love with Matt, she had harbored a secret crush on Dusty. His wide green eyes were clear panes of sensitivity, yet the rest of his face was as inscrutable as a blank page. He was one of those rare guys it was impossible to categorize. Even Matt, for all his eccentric behavior, was an open book next to Dusty. The crush was still there, she supposed, not that it would have mattered to Dusty. He had never shown the slightest romantic interest in her or any girl that she knew of. "Aren't you going to ask me what's bothering me?" she asked miserably.

"If you want me to."

"How come you're not nosy like the rest of us?"

He showed a faint smile. "What's bothering you? Is it Matt?"

"Yes. But I can't tell you the specifics. It's too painful." She lowered her voice. "I think he hates me."

"Love turns to hate."

"Who said that?"

"Somebody wise. I don't remember who."

"Do you think it's true?" she asked.

He shrugged. "For a lot of people. But not for you and Matt. Why would he hate you?"

She hesitated. It was odd how Dusty's closed nature made her want to open up to him. In that moment she felt closer to him than anyone.

"Because I'm not good enough for him," she whispered.

"What are you talking about? What did he say to you?"

"Goodbye."

"Just goodbye?"

"Essentially." She gestured helplessly. "Can you believe that?"

He reached out and touched her arm. She would like to have said the gesture comforted her, but his fingers were strangely cold.

"People's moods change," he said. "He'll probably want you back tomorrow."

"He told me this last week."

"Then he'll probably want you back next week."

She had to smile. Yet the smile didn't last. "He might want somebody next week, but I don't think it will be me."

"I think you're wrong, Sheila. I don't think this is over yet. Where is he going to find someone as pretty as you?"

He had never called her pretty before. The remark made her feel slightly better, but talking about Matt had really depressed her. She didn't know why she had brought him up in the first place.

"What about you?" she asked. "How come I never see you with anybody pretty, pretty boy?"

It was Dusty's turn to be sad, and she worried that she might have offended him. "My relationships with girls are usually brief."

"You just haven't found the right girl. Hey, can I tell you a secret? You have to swear to me you won't tell a soul."

Dusty looked as if her telling him the big secret

would make not the slightest difference in his day. "All right," he said quietly.

"You know my friend Nancy? I think she likes you."

He paused. "Nancy who?"

"Nancy Bardella, the best-looking girl in this class, next to me, of course. Dummy, you know Nancy. She sits up front." Sheila paused. "She's not here today."

Dusty followed her gaze. "It doesn't look like it."

"That's weird, she told me she had a lot of stuff to get done in lab today."

"Maybe she got sick."

"I talked to her last night. She wasn't sick then."

Dusty shook his head. "I don't know."

"Her parents are supposed to be away for a few days." She added, "I hope she's all right."

Dusty stared at her. "Yeah."

"I think I better give her a call at lunch. Anyway, what do you think about what I just said?"

"I'm sorry?"

"About Nancy liking you?"

"I'm surprised.

"Why don't you ask her out?"

"I couldn't do that."

"Why not?"

He spoke with odd certainty, but also very softly, as if he wanted no one else to hear his words. "Nancy and I are never going out."

Ten minutes later class ended, and their test

tubes were still bubbling foul-smelling gases. She collected her books and headed for the parking lot. She had only four classes and was able to leave at lunch if she wanted, although she often stayed late to study in the library because she found it impossible to do any serious work at home with her younger brother's fascination with loud heavy metal. Ted really did dress as if he wanted to be on MTV.

Matt, her ex, her true love, the bane of her existence, just happened to be walking to the same part of the parking lot as she was. It wasn't coincidence because she had made a point of parking next to his car that morning. A million times during the week she had sworn to herself that she wasn't going to talk to him, that she was going to give herself a chance to heal, but the wound inside her chest was bleeding so profusely, she doubted it would ever close unless she cleared up some things first. At the same time she knew talking would clear up nothing, that she would feel worse after she saw him. Just spotting him in the parking lot made her feel sick to her stomach. He looked so good, his hair flowing over his shoulders, his black silk shirt with the top three buttons undone, his tan chest. How she used to love to move her hands over his hard belly. But she kept walking toward him because the thread of pain that bound her to him was too taut to pull back on. She felt as if she were going to snap every minute since he had dumped her.

"Hi, Sheila," he said.

Ah, that hurt, how casual he sounded when she couldn't have spelled the word *casual* had she been spotted the first five letters. He even had a smile on his face, and she would have hated him for that as well if the smile hadn't been so beautiful. She wanted desperately to kiss that smile, to know he was smiling because he was happy to see her. But that wasn't the case, and it never would be again. "I don't feel the same anymore, Sheila." There was no going back from that. No one ever felt the same once love was dead, and she didn't care what happened in movies and books. Once love died it was dead. Still, though, she kept walking toward him, hoping that everything she knew was wrong, that he would tell her he missed her, that he wanted her back.

"Hi," she said, stepping between their cars. He was close, five feet away. If she fainted while they spoke he could reach her before she hit the ground. But what if they didn't speak? What if he just said hi and drove away? That would probably be best, she thought, even though she knew it would be the worst. "How are you?" she asked.

"Fine," he said. "How are you?"

"Good."

"You look good."

"Thanks. So do you."

"You don't have to be good to look it," he said.

"Something your grandfather always said?"

"Something somebody said." He opened his car door. This was it. He was going to leave and she was going to faint and there would be no one to catch her. She would hit her head and have a cerebral hemorrhage and fall into a coma and wake up in the year 2047. Matt would be an old fart and she would still look like a babe, and he would realize he had blown it when he had dumped her. Boy, would he regret it.

"Are you going?" she asked, a tad pitifully. He was only opening the passenger door.

"I was just setting my stuff down," he said. Giving her a worried glance, he dropped his book and pen in the front seat. Then he was staring at her again, and that was the hardest part, seeing his eyes, knowing he knew she was about to burst into tears. He spoke carefully. "How are you really, Sheila?" he asked.

She burst out crying. God, how stupid, she thought, how useless. Sure, now he was standing close to her, his arms around her, cooing soft things in her ear. She didn't want his sympathy, she didn't want his concern. She wanted his love and she couldn't buy that with tears. She didn't know what God charged for that little thing, but she knew the price was constantly changing.

"I'm here," he was saying. "It's all right."

She sniffed. "It's not all right. It's horrible." She pulled back. "I have to go. I shouldn't have parked here. I can't see you."

He grabbed her arm. "Sheila. Wait. I have to talk to you."

She was instantly hopeful. No, not really, her hope was so laced with despair it could have been made of toxic waste; it was really no hope at all. Yet she suddenly found herself waiting with terrible expectation for what he would say next.

"What?" she asked, wiping at her face.

"I miss you," he said.

"Yeah?" She didn't want him to add anything. Just, I miss you, Sheila. Then she could fill in the rest. I love you, Sheila. I want to be with you, Sheila. I want to kiss you, Sheila. Please take me back, Sheila.

"But I think this is for the best," he continued.

She swallowed thickly. "What is *this?*"

He hesitated. "Our breaking up. I think it's best for both of us." He could see he wasn't scoring any points and reached out to touch her again. "What I mean is, I feel awful and I'm sure you feel awful, but I think in the long run we'll both do better because of this." He stopped himself and she was glad for the small favor. He studied her face, which must have truly been a sight, and then shrugged. "I'm sorry," he said.

"The long run," she whispered.

"Pardon?"

"I was just thinking that when we were in love it was enough to be 'in the moment' with each other." She coughed. "But that was when we were in love."

"I still love you, Sheila. We can still be friends."

They had discussed these things already. She had read how, when people broke up, their subsequent conversations usually went in circles. Because really, there was nothing to say if one wanted to leave and the other wanted to stay. It was all doomed. She took a step back from him.

"You love me but you're not in love with me," she said. "We cannot be friends. I cannot stand to be with you partially when I used to have you totally." She couldn't stop crying. "Can't you see that, Matt?"

He tried to hug her again but she wouldn't let him. He continued to stare at her with concern. She almost wished he was more insensitive, that he was a jerk so she could feel furious with him.

"I understand," he said. "If it hurts too much to see me, I'll keep my distance." He paused. "If that's what you really want."

"What do you really want?"

"To continue seeing you."

"But would I be your girlfriend then?" What a pitiful question. Yet she hoped he would avoid giving her a direct answer because she knew the truth would hurt too much. And it did.

He shook his head. "No."

Her face broke. "Just, no? Don't you want to think about it?"

Another bad question. But she asked it because she had this idea that if she did start seeing him again, spent time with him, his heart would open to her again and he would come back.

"Sheila"—he spread his arms—"what can I say?"

"Say you've been going through a terrible phase and you're out of it now and that you realize that you gave up the best thing you ever had when you gave me up."

"Sheila."

"Say you made a mistake. That this is all wrong and we can go back to the way it was. No, just say, 'I love you, Sheila. I love you I love you I love you. And I don't care about anything else except that I love you.' " She had to stop to take a breath, to sob. "Just say something, for God's sake, other than no. I can't stand to hear you tell me no."

He got his arms around her again. She lowered her head while he kissed the side of her face, his skin cool against her hot tears. Suddenly her head was aching as if it were wedged in a nutcracker. The pain was so intense, she wondered if she'd be able to drive home.

"What should we do?" he asked finally, softly, in her ear. "What can I do to help you, Sheila?"

"Love me," she whispered.

"I love you."

She raised her head and knew she should just leave it at that. He said he loved her, and even though she knew everything was ruined, she would try to remember only that so she could make it to the next day and not die. On top of having a headache, she felt sick to her stomach, exhausted. She leaned forward and kissed his cheek.

"You were a great boyfriend, Matt," she mumbled.

"You were a great girlfriend."

She nodded. "Yeah." She turned away. "I have to go."

He stopped her. "Are you sure you can drive?"

She hesitated. She wanted to say yes, which was probably the truth. But if she said no, he would offer to take her home, and she could be with him a few minutes more, and maybe during that time he would look at her and the old love . . . No, she had to stop thinking that way. Yet she didn't want to leave him this minute. God, did she want to stay with him.

"I have a bad headache," she said.

He took her arm. "Come on, I'll take you home. We can always get your car later. You shouldn't be alone at a time like this."

She let herself be led into the front seat of his car, a brand-new 626 Mazda, red as her bloodshot eyes, bought with money made from mixed drinks. She had never liked the fact that Matt was a bartender, but her likes and dislikes were academic at this point.

They didn't talk much on the way to her house. But she did remark that Nancy hadn't been at school that day, though.

"Maybe she's sick," he said.

"That's what Dust said, but I don't know."

"Dust?"

"Dusty Shame. He's my lab partner in chemistry. You know him."

"I didn't know his nickname." He nodded. "He's a strange guy."

"What's strange about him? I like him."

"I don't know, there's just something about him that's not right. Did you know his mother has Alzheimer's? He lives alone with her. She's a complete vegetable."

A note of disapproval entered her voice. "He did tell me about his mom once, but he said she was a flower, not a vegetable. And I don't think you can say someone's strange just because his mother's sick."

"That's not what I meant."

"What did you mean?" She wasn't used to snapping at him like this, but supposed it went along with their being "just friends."

Matt shrugged. "Nothing."

"I had a crush on Dust once."

"Yeah? I had a crush on Nancy once."

God, that hurt, and she knew she deserved it. "You didn't have to say that, Matt."

"You were the one who started it." He stopped. "Look, let's drop it."

"I want to swing by Nancy's house," she said suddenly.

"Why?"

"It's only a few minutes out of the way."

"But you can call her when you get home."

Sheila didn't respond immediately. She didn't know why she had said what she had, about going by Nancy's, the words just popped out of her mouth. Yet she realized at that minute that she had been worried about Nancy since she noticed she wasn't in class.

"I need to see her," she said. "If she's sick I won't be able to drive over and see her without my car."

"Do you want to go back to get your car?"

"No," Sheila said. "I told you what I want. Can you do me this one little favor? Hell, maybe you can ask her out while we're there. She's always told me what a great body you have." She winced at her own remark. "I'm sorry."

Matt concentrated on the road. "We seem to be saying that a lot these days. I accept your apology." He added, "We can go by Nancy's."

"Thank you."

At the Bardellas', Sheila rang the bell a number of times but got no answer. Matt stood beside her on the porch, beads of sweat on his forehead. It was a hellish day, she thought, in a lot of ways. Nancy's house belonged to one of the new tracts, which she hated. They were springing up everywhere, as if developers wouldn't be satisfied until all of southern California were paved over.

"She must have decided to ditch," Matt said.

"Nancy never ditched in her life."

"Maybe she decided to go with her parents. Where did you say they went?"

"To Las Vegas," Sheila said. "Her father has to work at an engineering trade show. But Nancy wouldn't have gone. Vegas bores her, and besides, she told me last night she had a ton of work to catch up on at school."

"So she went out. Big deal."

"I want to look in the garage to see if her car's there."

"There are no windows in their garage. How can you look?"

She stepped off the porch. "I'll go down on my hands and knees and peek under the garage door."

He followed her. "What's gotten into you, Sheila?"

"It must be the heat."

Her squinting under the garage door proved to her that Nancy's car was there. She sat back on the clean concrete, the heat of the driveway burning her butt, Matt standing above her.

"That's odd," she said thoughtfully.

"So she went out with someone else," Matt said. "Or else you're wrong and she went with her parents. I don't understand why you're so worried."

She got up slowly, ignoring Matt's offered hand. "I want to break in to see if she's inside."

"What? That's crazy. How are we going to break in? And why?"

"She might be there and too sick to answer the door. She might have fallen and hurt herself. I don't know, I'm just worried about her and I can't explain it. Let's hop over the wall and find an open window."

Matt scrutinized her five and a half foot height, and shook his head. "I'll hop over the wall. You wait here."

He opened the front door of the house five minutes later. She stepped inside quickly, feeling the air-conditioning. "Is she here?" she asked.

"I called out," Matt said. "No one's here."

"Did you look upstairs?" she asked, scanning the living room area, glancing toward the family room. There was a feeling in the house—she couldn't put a finger on it. Sort as if something had recently been sucked out of it. Yes, she thought, the house felt emptied of life.

"No," Matt said. "I was in a hurry to let you inside."

"Nancy!" she called. "Nancy!" She moved toward the steps. "Let's go to her bedroom."

Nancy's room was empty, the bed had obviously been hastily made. This did nothing to settle Sheila's mind. She had known Nancy since they were little, and she was always very tidy. She never made the bed without tucking in the edges. Sheila said as much to Matt and he thought she was being ridiculous.

It was then they noticed the card lying on top of the bed.

Sheila picked it up with Matt studying it over her shoulder.

It was white.

And had a black swastika on it.

"What the hell is this?" Sheila muttered.

"That's a swastika," Matt said. "It was Nazi Germany's symbol in World War Two."

"I know that. I meant what's it doing here on her bed?"

For the first time Matt appeared to be uneasy. "Nancy's not doing a report on the Nazis for school?"

"No." Sheila scanned the rest of the room. Nancy usually left her purse on top of her desk, but her desk was clear. "I wonder if there's a way I can get hold of her parents in Vegas. Let's check by the phone downstairs, see if there's a number."

The Bardellas kept a notepad on the wall next to the phone in the kitchen. Fortunately, there did appear to be a number where her parents were staying—the Tropicana—800-555-4000. Sheila dialed the number and asked for the Bardellas' room. It rang only once before Nancy's mother picked up.

"Hello?"

"Mrs. Bardella? This is Sheila."

"How are you, Sheila?" The woman sounded pleased. She had always been like a second mom to Sheila.

"Good, I think. I was just wondering if Nancy was with you in Vegas?"

"No, Nancy had school today." She paused. "Didn't you see her?"

"She wasn't there. And I'm at your house now and she's not here, either."

"You're at our house? How did you get in?"

"We broke in. My boyfriend—Matt is here with me. I'm sorry, I was worried about Nancy. Her car is here. Did she say anything to you about going somewhere with somebody?"

"No." There was concern in Mrs. Bardella's voice now and Sheila felt guilty for worrying the woman. "Nancy never ditches school."

"I know," Sheila said. She wasn't going to bring up the swastika card. "Look, it's probably nothing. For all I know she's just gone out for a walk. I'll call around to our friends and see if I can find her."

"Could you do that, dear? And call me back as soon as you can? I'll wait here."

"Sure."

They said their goodbyes and Sheila set down the phone. Matt sat at the kitchen table. "She's not in Vegas?" he asked.

"No." Sheila fingered the card in her hand. "I think I should call the police."

"What about trying her other friends, like you told Nancy's mother?"

"Our friends are still at school. And none of them are into Nazis." She picked up the phone again. "Should I dial nine-one-one?"

"That's what they taught us in elementary school," Matt muttered.

Nine-one-one was no number to call in an emergency. They put Sheila on hold for fifteen minutes before a bored-sounding woman got back to her. Halfway through her explanation of the situation,

Sheila was interrupted and transferred to a bored-sounding gentleman. She had to start over with her story. She wasn't even sure if the man was taking notes or what. When she was done, he told her a person had to be missing a minimum of twenty-four hours before he could file a missing person's report.

"But she could be in danger," Sheila protested. "In twenty-four hours she could be dead."

"That's unlikely," the man replied. "It sounds as if your friend could be shopping at the mall."

"But what about the swastika card? Nancy would never leave a thing like that lying around."

"I can't comment on that. I don't know your friend."

"Well, I do. Listen, are you a cop?"

"A police officer? No, I am not."

"Let me talk to an officer."

"I'm afraid that's not possible."

"Why not?"

"This is an emergency line and your situation does not warrant emergency attention." He paused. "I'm sorry, but if you knew how many calls we get a day, you'd understand. In ninety-nine out of a hundred cases the person shows up before the day is through. But if you like, I can do a traffic accident check on your friend to see if she shows up on any of our reports."

Sheila didn't know what to say. "Thanks. Call me at this number if you find out anything. What's your name in case I want to get back to you?"

"Dean Nan. You can request me personally. I'll be here until five this afternoon."

"Thanks, Mr. Nan."

"Try not to worry," he said.

"Yeah." Sheila said goodbye and set the phone down. Matt was watching her. "I think I should stay here in case the police call back, or Nancy shows up. There's no reason you have to stay, though."

Matt shrugged. "I don't mind hanging out with you."

She closed her eyes and sighed. "Why this on top of everything else?"

"Nancy will probably come walking in that door in the next couple of hours."

Sheila opened her eyes. "But even if she does, you'll still not be my boyfriend." It was a selfish thing to say, with her friend's safety in doubt, but she couldn't help herself. Matt understood that. He didn't respond.

They were sitting in the family room not ten minutes later when the phone rang. The man on the other end identified himself as Lieutenant Black of the Los Angeles Police Department. Sheila had not called the L.A.P.D., but its San Bernadino counterpart since Chino was a part of San Bernadino. Lt. Black sounded young but authoritative. He wanted to hear about Nancy Bardella.

She repeated her story, which wasn't much of a story. But she didn't have to be psychic to know which part of the tale interested Lt. Black—it was the swastika card. He had her describe it to him in detail, and then fell silent for a long period when she was done.

"Have you had a card like this pop up in other missing person situations?" Sheila finally asked.

"I am not at liberty to release that information," he said smoothly. "Have you personally handled the card?"

"Yes. My boyfriend— A friend and I both have." She paused. "Are you worried about fingerprints?"

"We would prefer the scene be left as undisturbed as possible. You say you're in Chino? I want the address. I'm coming there immediately. Also, I prefer that you touch nothing else, no matter how insignificant. Could you do that for me, Sheila?"

"Yes. But please answer at least this question for me. Do you think my friend is in danger?"

He didn't hesitate. "Yes."

They must have had experience with the swastika card before. "Should I call her parents and have them return home?" she asked.

"Where are they?"

"Las Vegas. The Tropicana Hotel. Nancy's mother is waiting for a call from me now."

"I'll call them. They should return home immediately."

"Oh, God," Sheila whispered. "Do you think Nancy's dead?"

"Let's not talk about that at this stage. I'll be there in fifty minutes. Sit tight."

The lieutenant got off the line. Sheila staggered over to the couch and plopped down beside Matt. "What is it?" he asked anxiously.

"The police must have an M.O. on who was here."

"A what?"

"A *modus operandi.* A mode of operation."

"They recognized the card?"

"Yes."

"Did they say where they had seen it before?"

"No." She was trembling. "But I have a feeling it was in bad places."

Lieutenant Black arrived fifty minutes later. He was alone, but indicated he had back-up coming soon. He was approximately thirty-five, with a head of full brown hair, blue eyes, and a tan chiseled jaw. His dark sport coat was cut expensively. He, in fact, resembled a handsome TV cop, and for some reason that reassured Sheila—that they had a real hero to help them. He shook both their hands quickly before moving up to the bedroom. His eyes were everywhere. He wanted to know how they had gotten in the house, if they had a key. Matt explained about the back window, how he had popped it open with his car keys. Lt. Black wasn't happy about that. He hurried back downstairs, with them on his heels. Matt showed him the window he had used; it was the only one that was open, he explained. Lt. Black knelt and studied it without touching it.

"The metal is slightly bent," he muttered.

"I might have done that," Matt confessed.

Black glanced at him. "Maybe you did."

Sheila understood. "Or maybe the person who came for Nancy did it?"

Lt. Black didn't answer. He stood. "Where's the card?"

She led him to the kitchen, where she had left it face-up on the table. The swastika was only on one side; the other was completely blank. The design was so symmetrical that Sheila assumed it had been bought already printed. But now, as she studied it more closely, she realized it was drawn. She mentioned that to Lt. Black and he nodded.

"And you've seen it before," Sheila said. "Don't deny it, I can tell. What does it mean? Who left it?"

"I don't know what it means," Lt. Black said, "other than a reference to Nazi Germany. And I don't know who left it. I'm telling you the truth."

"But you have seen it in other missing person cases?" Sheila asked, her voice unsteady.

"I'm not at liberty to discuss that." He raised his hand as they started to protest. "I know I sound like a bureaucratic ass, but understand, Nancy's parents have not even been fully apprised of the situation. When they arrive, maybe I can say more. They have already given us permission to complete a full investigation of the crime scene."

She sucked in a breath at his mention of the word *crime.* "What are you looking for?" she asked.

He sighed, and in the gesture it was also clear to Sheila that he had been working on the case long before Nancy had disappeared. He sat down at the kitchen table and wearily put his hands to his head.

"Anything," he said.

3

At the time that Sheila Hardholt and Matthew Jaye were waiting for Mr. and Mrs. Bardella to return home, Dusty Shame sat at his computer in his bedroom and searched for victim number four. He had subscribed to the computer service *Einstein* two years earlier because he was interested in many of the services it had to offer—access to a large encyclopedia, immediate updates on important news items, open forum discussions on a wide variety of subjects—not because he planned to use it to select girls to kill to quiet the voice in his head. But *Einstein* had turned out to be his safest access to information about young females.

The billboards on the computer network allowed him to meet people via electronic mail, or E-mail as it was called. *Einstein* offered a place where numerous topics could be discussed and debated: books, fiction and nonfiction; movies; music; stars; politics; science. Dusty combed these categories searching for young voices, innocent voices, that would satisfy the very old voice in his brain.

Making contact was easy. For example, he had found his first victim, the witty Stacy Domino in the music section. She was a devoted Led Zeppelin fan and had actually founded the billboard club devoted to that rock group. Dusty had read her notes for a month, noting her particular obsession with Jimmy Page, the guitarist, before he sent her a private E-mail. That was one thing he was careful about. He never posted a public note in any billboard club.

Stacy had responded promptly, as he knew she would. He had introduced himself as a budding electric guitarist who was equally obsessed with Jimmy Page's heavy riffs. They exchanged E-mail for a month and during that time he learned a great deal about Stacy and her household. Yet she learned nothing about him, even though when she was alive, she would have thought differently.

His registration with the *Einstein* service was under a false name, and the post office box they sent his bill to had been registered using a false ID. Yeah, he had not intended to use the network to search for victims, but even at the beginning he must have known he'd use it for something destructive.

In either case Stacy thought his name was William Wand, and that he had a used Les Paul guitar that cost five thousand and change, and that he slept with it at night, with headphones on playing Zeppelin's box set at a subliminal volume. This was so he was always in the Zep vibe, always ready to jam. But he had taught her just how rough a heavy metal jam could be that night when she was alone. That dark night she had sent him a sexy E-mail note, telling him how much she wished he could be there with her. That *very* dark night he had smashed in her skull with his heavy metal hammer.

And the irony was he hated Led Zeppelin.

At present he was focusing in on a prime candidate for his next murder. Her name was Wendy Bart and he had found her in the book section under horror. She was a huge Stephen King and Peter Straub fan. He had gone out and bought a few of each of their books so he could converse sensibly with her over the modem lines. The disturbed characters in the novels had not affected him in the slightest. It wasn't as if they were like him, he thought. He couldn't relate to them in any but a superficial manner. He knew one thing few novelists knew about people like himself—they could not be explained by events in their past. The memory of pain was not pain. His pain, his disturbance, existed in the moment. It was just that for him every blessed moment seemed to take forever.

Still, his life had been very unhappy.

He hated to admit that to himself sometimes.

Maybe the authors knew more than he thought.

He was exhausted already, and he had just done

Nancy, and the voice was already back, telling him to kill again. He had tried to take a nap that afternoon, but it had been in vain. The whispered words in his head simply would not stop. He knew he had a goal. The voices had told him. He hoped it was more of a finish than just a momentary goal. He had to get to number six. Six innocents. There was a special significance to that number, at least as far as the voice was concerned. He wondered if it had to do with the remains he had found in the cave. There had been six distinct graves in the dry sands.

He was thinking of trying to kill Wendy Bart that night.

Her parents weren't going out of town, but they were going to be home late, long after Wendy should be in bed. That was not the coincidence it appeared since he was in tentative communication with close to fifty young women, all of whom lived in southern California. Where they lived was the primary criterion he used in selecting a victim. Wendy had told him her parents' schedule with her last E-mail note. He had printed out a copy of it.

> Dear William,
>
> I think I have become addicted to talking to you, and I've never even heard your voice. I loved your last note and agree with you about your observations on King's latest books versus his early ones. Except for one thing—I think *The Tommyknockers* was as

good as anything he's ever done, and that includes *The Shining* and *Pet Sematary.* I love how he does a drunk. You know the Jim Gardener character in *The Tommyknockers,* he sounded so genuine. King must have been drunk more than a few times in his life, I'd guess. The same can't be said for me. The most I've ever had to drink at one time was two beers, and all it did was make me throw up. I told you I was a wimp. Honestly, I'm no one to fantasize about, even though I have to admit I have a few fantasies about you. Too bad you live on the other side of the country or I'd invite you over tomorrow night, Friday. My parents are going to an awards banquet in San Diego and won't be back till the wee hours. I'd love to get together with you, make a big bowl of popcorn, and watch horror videos all night. I do love those old black-and-white sci flicks like *Them* and *The Thing.* They just don't make stuff like that now. I know we'd have a blast.

Well, I'd better go. Keep in touch. Watch out for the bogeyman.

OOOXXX Wendy

Wendy Bart, probably following her parents' advice from an early age, had never revealed her address, and he hadn't pressed her for it. There was no need because it was listed in the phone book. He had already been to her house and observed her through a pair of powerful binoculars from a distance of approximately two hundred yards. He knew Wendy drove a brown Honda Civic, had long blond hair, had no brothers or sisters, and limped slightly, as if her right knee had been injured. She was a big girl, maybe five eight, one hundred and thirty pounds, roughly sixteen to eighteen years old. He also knew, from her notes and her appearance, that she was a sweet girl, and that the voice would be pleased if she was killed.

Her house was in Pasadena, the other side of Los Angeles. Since she was such a video buff, it was conceivable that she'd stay up late watching movies until her parents returned from San Diego. But he doubted it, from the tone of her note. Her house was also located on a quiet cul-de-sac, like Nancy's. He believed that that night might be the perfect opportunity to get in, smash Wendy's brain, get rid of the body, and then have a nice long sleep. He needed rest as an addict needs a fix.

Why hadn't the murder of Nancy calmed the voice for a few days?

Why hadn't it been like before?

He didn't know.

But he had this fear that soon there would be nothing he could do to stop it. That it would always be there, until he blew his brains out.

Something touched his shoulder from behind.

Dusty whirled around, his heart in his mouth.

Blank, sunken eyes stared down at him.

"Mom," he gasped.

She had wandered into his bedroom and caught him off-guard. He was surprised her had not heard her approach, never mind smelled her approach. His mother always had a dank air about her, no matter how many times she was bathed. Her eyes drifted from him to Wendy's note lying on his desk beside his computer screen. Her expression remained unchanged. Her lined hand continued to rest on his shoulder. Dusty couldn't be free of the feeling that it was actually a huge insect that had landed on him, and not his dear mother's hand. He had been dreaming about insects a lot lately, cockroaches in particular, thinking how they probably eventually worked their way through the plastic bags he had placed his victims in. He imagined they would eat the eyes first. He'd had a dream about how Nancy had come crying to him, with bloody tears, blaming him because she couldn't find her eyeballs. It had not been a restful night.

"How are you doing, Mom?" he asked, lifting her hand up and letting her arm fall to her side. How much like a puppet she was, he thought, as he watched the dangling limb swing back and forth for a moment before it came to rest. How much like a puppet he was, pulled this way and that by a force he couldn't control. Not for the first time, he wondered what was the source of the voice, what gave it its power.

His mother coughed.

"Her name's Wendy," he said, nodding to the girl's note on his desk. "She seems like a good choice for what comes next."

His mother continued to watch him.

"She's a big fan of books," he said. "Mainly horror novels. She loves to be scared, she says. But I don't know if she knows what she's been talking about because I can't see how a bunch of words on paper could scare anybody."

His mother swayed a bit, from right to left.

"I don't know how old she is," he said. "She wouldn't tell me her age. That usually means someone's younger than she wants you to think. But I didn't tell her much about myself. She has a cat she's named Galadriel after the Elven queen in *The Lord of the Rings.* I'm glad she doesn't have a dog. Dogs are always a problem. In a way, they're a lot harder to take care of than people."

His mother blinked.

Dusty took a deep breath, wiping the sweat from his forehead. "But she's a nice girl. I've been writing to her for the last month. She reminds me of Nancy in a way. She never has anything bad to say about anybody." He smiled. "When she grows up she wants to be a doctor and work in a foreign mission. There aren't a lot of people like that around nowadays."

His mother began to drool.

Dusty felt his eyes burn. "She wants to go to

Stanford when she graduates from high school. She says she thinks she'll be accepted, that it's been a dream of hers all her life. Her mother went there, I guess. She really loves her mother. I can tell by the way she talks about her." A tear fell over his cheek. "She says that her mother is her inspiration." Dusty bowed his head and sobbed. "Oh, Mom," he whispered. "I *hate* this."

He didn't know how long he sat there crying before he noticed that his mother had reached out and touched the top of his head. He hardly recognized the touch because it felt nothing like that of an insect, nothing like an old comatose woman's. Her fingers on his scalp reminded him of when he had been a boy, and she had soothed his bruised feelings by running her fingers through his hair and telling him he was the best boy in the whole world. He raised his head, careful not to let her hand fall from his head. But it did anyway, and once more the arm swung by her side like that of a limb on a lifeless doll.

"Mom?" he said, studying her face.

There was no reaction. No one home.

Dusty turned around and switched off his computer. It was six o'clock, too early to head for Wendy's. But suddenly he couldn't stand the thought of remaining in the house a moment longer. He considered driving down to the beach, trying to fall asleep on the sand beside the roar of the ocean. Maybe the tide would come up while he rested and catch him unaware and wash away all his problems. He picked up his keys and stuffed them in his pocket. His *tools* were already in the car. He stood and kissed his mother on the cheek.

"Don't wait up for me," he said.

He left her there, staring into nothingness.

4

Sheila and Matt were on their way back to the Bardellas' after spending several hours waiting in a coffee shop. When Lt. Black's associates had arrived, the two of them had been politely told to leave the house. Lt. Black had called in a regular team. Before they left, Sheila watched as one man dusted for prints, while another combed for threads, and still another searched the backyard. The thoroughness of their investigation did nothing to calm Sheila. It told her that they were dealing with an enemy the police had met before—and failed to stop.

Sheila drank eight cups of coffee at the coffee shop. Matt sat and read last week's sports page. Lt. Black said they could come back when Nancy's parents arrived. Sheila was able to estimate when they would arrive by how far away Las Vegas was.

So there they were, pulling once more onto Nancy's street.

"That's her parents' car," Sheila said, pointing to the Lexus in the driveway.

"They must have done a hundred all the way," Matt said.

"Yeah."

"It was nice of the lieutenant to let us return."

"He probably wants to question us more about Nancy—who she was seeing and stuff like that."

"Was Nancy seeing anybody?" Matt asked.

"No."

"Did she seem concerned about anything?"

"Only about her grade in chemistry," Sheila said.

Nancy's mom met them at the door, and the sight of her jolted Sheila. The woman was petite, always well dressed, a member of numerous clubs and organizations founded to enrich Chino. She had aged ten years since Sheila had seen her last. Mr. Bardella was in the kitchen with Lt. Black. No father had ever loved his daughter more than Mr. Bardella. He was a strong man ordinarily. Now, though, he looked like a house that lost its foundation and collapsed in upon itself. A bottle of whiskey sat in front of him on the kitchen table now. He nodded as they entered but didn't look up.

"Sheila, Matt," Lt. Black said in welcome. He stood quickly and offered Sheila his chair. He grabbed one from the corner for Nancy's mother, then leaned against the counter with Matt by his side. The rest of the team appeared to have left. Having Lt. Black present helped to steady the room. He radiated authority, competence. All their eyes were on him. A moment of silence went by while he gathered his thoughts.

"This is a grave situation," he began. "I will not pretend otherwise. But before I begin, do I have your permission, Mr. and Mrs. Bardella, to talk about this matter in front of Sheila and Matt?"

"Yes," Nancy's mother said. Her father nodded. Sheila could smell the alcohol on his breath.

"What I say now must remain confidential," Lt. Black said. "This information was not in the papers. There are certain facts, such as the swastika card, that we must keep private so that when we do apprehend who is behind this, we will know for certain that we don't have an imposter on our hands—someone who might want to confess to a crime he hasn't committed. Does everyone understand?"

They all understood. Lt. Black cleared his throat.

"We believe Nancy has been kidnapped," he began. "This is the third situation we have seen like this in the last five weeks. The item that provides a definite connection between them is the swastika card. But there are other particulars. The previous two girls were abducted while their parents were away for the night. The perpetrator entered through a back window."

"But I came through the window when I broke in," Matt said.

"We know that," Lt. Black said. "We have taken that into account. Trust me when I say you weren't the first one through that window, and that the tool this person used to open it is the same tool he used to open the previous two windows." He paused. "Like Nancy, the other two girls appear to have been taken unaware while they slept. Then, after subduing them in a manner we are not yet sure of, the kidnapper hastily made the beds and removed a few small items from the bedroom: purses, makeup kits, things like that. This was to give the impression that the girls might have left home."

"But why would the kidnapper leave a card if he was trying to create that illusion?" Matt asked.

"We don't believe he's serious about creating the illusion," Lt. Black said. "It seems he does it as a matter of course, in an offhanded way. There are other things that connect these three disappearances. At the scene of each, and here today, we found traces of light brown hair that doesn't match that of anyone in any of the three households. We have also found size nine footprints outside each window that was used to gain entrance to the three houses."

"Have you found any fingerprints?" Mr. Bardella asked.

"No," Lt. Black said. "We believe the kidnapper wears gloves. We're not sure what type of vehicle he drives, but have received reports of a suspicious small car in the neighborhood the nights of the first two kidnappings."

"A small car?" Mr. Bardella asked as if they couldn't do better than that.

"That's all we have on the vehicle at this time,"

Lt. Black said. "But we'll be going around the neighborhood and asking if anyone can expand upon this description for us. Let me go on. Each of the girls abducted was of high school age, sixteen through eighteen. All live in this general area, but scattered about—one from Orange County, another from L.A. County, and now Nancy, who lives here in San Bernadino County. We don't know what else connects these girls. I am going to ask you all a few questions before I leave that I hope will shed some light on why they were chosen. But we do feel the kidnapper must have known each of them in some way to know that they would be alone the nights they were kidnapped."

"That's logical," Sheila said.

"But I don't understand," Mrs. Bardella broke in, her mouth twitching as she spoke. "You keep calling these kidnappings and the person who took our girl a kidnapper. But aren't there usually ransom notes in kidnappings?"

"Yes," Lt. Black said reluctantly. "But it often happens that the notes take time to arrive."

"Have you received any notes on the first two girls?" Mrs. Bardella asked.

"No."

"Oh God," Mrs. Bardella whispered. Her husband took her hand. The woman began to cry softly. Sheila felt tears burning her eyes, but didn't want to break down in front of Nancy's mother. She understood what the lieutenant was saying. He was calling them kidnappings because the word carried hope with it. But he didn't believe they were.

"Were there any signs of violence at any of the girls' houses?" Mr. Bardella asked softly.

"No overt signs," Lt. Black said. "But at the second girl's house we found a drop of blood on her bed sheet. It was later confirmed to be her blood type."

Mr. Bardella was pale. "Just one drop?"

"Yes," Lt. Black said.

"Did you find any blood in Nancy's room?" Mr. Bardella asked.

"Not yet," Lt. Black said.

"But you're still looking?" Mr. Bardella asked.

"Yes," Lt. Black said.

"Because you have reason to believe the girls may have been hurt before they were abducted?" Mr. Bardella asked, continuing to torture himself.

"Yes," Lt. Black said. He added, "I am sorry."

Mr. Bardella let go of his wife's hand and buried his face in his own hands. The pain in the room was so thick, it was a wonder the walls did not weep. Lt. Black may have radiated authority, but he had no good news to tell them. Mrs. Bardella asked the question they were all afraid to ask.

"Do you think Nancy could be dead?"

Lt. Black drew in a breath. "I honestly can't say. Since the other two girls have been taken, we have been unable to find a single trace of them."

"No one has contacted you?" Mrs. Bardella asked.

"No."

"There has been no demand for ransom?" Mrs. Bardella asked, for the second time.

"No."

"The girls are just gone?" Sheila blurted out, unable to contain herself.

"They may be fine," Lt. Black said. "There are many possibilities still left to us. We must proceed under the assumption we are going to find them safe and well."

"Do you have any more clues as to what this guy looks like?" Matt asked. "Besides his light brown hair and his size nine shoes?"

"We think he's young," Lt. Black said. "It's a logical deduction assuming that he knew each of the girls personally."

"But I'm Nancy's best friend," Sheila protested. "She didn't know any psychopaths. No one was bothering her. She would have told me. Look, this swastika card—could one of those neo-Nazi groups be involved?"

"We have been investigating the local chapters of these groups and plan to continue to investigate them. But so far we have turned up nothing."

"So you have no suspects?" Mr. Bardella asked.

"We have none at this time." Lt. Black removed a notepad and pen from his back pocket. "Let me get to these questions. Now I'm going to tell you the names of the first two girls who were abducted. This information is confidential—for obvious reasons. I am telling you their names to see if they ring a bell—if Nancy had ever mentioned them before. The first one is Stacy Domino. She lives in Orange County. She disappeared five weeks ago." He paused. "Have any of you heard this name before?"

None of them had. Sheila racked her brain and came up with nothing. She was sure she would have remembered Nancy talking about the girl. "Where exactly in Orange County does Stacy live?" Sheila asked.

"I can't give out that information without the permission of Stacy's father," Lt. Black said. "But I'll ask for it and get back to you if he says it's OK. There could be some value in all of you talking together. The second girl's name is Debra Weston. She lives in Los Angeles." He paused. "Did Nancy ever speak of her?"

Once more they came up empty. Lt. Black was disappointed and studied his notepad for a long time before asking his next questions.

"Was Nancy involved in drug use of any kind?"

"No," Mrs. Bardella said.

"No," Sheila said.

"She smoked pot occasionally," Matt said. They looked at him. He shrugged. "It was no big deal, but a few of my friends got loaded with her."

"Nancy would never use marijuana," Mr. Bardella said angrily.

"Please," Lt. Black interrupted smoothly. "I'm sure Matt would not invent the information, and I don't think it's important anyway. Let's continue. Did Nancy have a boyfriend?"

"No," Mrs. Bardella said.

"No," Sheila said.

"She had seen a friend of mine a few times," Matt said reluctantly.

"Who?" Sheila exclaimed.

"Danny Folgelson," Matt said.

"That guy's a creep," Sheila said. "She would have told me."

"I guess she didn't tell you everything," Matt said.

"This is interesting," Lt. Black said. "Are you saying that Nancy led a double life, Matt?"

"No," Matt said firmly. "She was just like everybody else. She had a few things going on in her life that she didn't talk about." He turned to Nancy's parents. "I apologize for bringing these things up. I'm just trying to give the lieutenant as much to go on as I can."

"There's no need to apologize," Mr. Bardella said. "I shouldn't have snapped at you." He glanced at Lt. Black. "Do you have any more questions?"

"The most important one," Lt. Black said. "Who knew Nancy would be alone last night?"

"Lots of kids," Sheila said. "I heard her talking in chemistry class about how her parents were going away for a few days and she'd have the whole house to herself."

"I told several of my friends that we were going away," Mrs. Bardella said.

"People at Hughes knew my wife and I were

going to be out of town for a few days," Mr. Bardella said. "Add all these people up, and that's a lot of leads to check out, Lieutenant."

"And we'll check them out," Lt. Black said evenly. "But for now I'm most interested in whom Nancy told that she was going to be alone. As I said, we believe we are searching for someone young, maybe even someone in high school."

"That sounds a little farfetched," Mr. Bardella said.

Lt. Black stared at him. "Why? In the barrios I have seen kids ten years old wield knives like pros." He turned back to Sheila. "I want a list of every student in your chemistry class."

"I don't know every student. But I can give you my teacher's name—Dan Spade. He lives here in Chino. I think he's in the phone book."

"Good." Lt. Black made a note on his pad. Then he closed it and put it in his back pocket. "I think that's enough for now. I'll be calling you later tonight to keep you updated on what is happening. As I mentioned, my people will be in the neighborhood trying to find anybody who may have seen something. I know this is a difficult time for all of you. I am at a loss as to what to say to present things in a better light, except that we at the L.A.P.D. are going to work until we have an answer." He removed four cards from his shirt pocket and gave each of them one. "This card has my home and work numbers on it, plus another number where a message can be left for me. I will be beeped immediately. Call if you remember anything that might be remotely useful. Call if you just want to talk. I am at your service twenty-four hours a day." He paused. He was really a good man, a sincere man. "I have a fourteen-year-old daughter, Mr. and Mrs. Bardella. I can imagine what you're going through."

Nancy's parents thanked him for his words, but their eyes told him that no one could imagine what they were going through. Lt. Black understood that. He hastily excused himself and said he could find his own way out. Sheila chased after him, and caught him in the driveway as he was getting into his car.

"I have to talk to you a moment," she said.

"Is there something you forgot to tell me?" he asked.

"Not exactly." She glanced about the neighborhood. The sun had set moments ago, soon it would be dark. A couple of Lt. Black's people could be seen going from door to door. Neighbors had come out of their houses and were staring at the Bardellas' residence. To think, they must have been saying, it happened next door to us. Poor Nancy, such a nice girl. Sheila knew the allure of tragedy that drew the people to stare, and hated it. "I want to help you find Nancy," she said.

"How do you want to help?" he asked.

"I want to be involved in the investigation."

He nodded. "You can help by talking to your friends in chemistry class and finding out where they were last night."

"None of my friends would have done this to Nancy."

"We have to explore every possible lead."

"All right, I'll check around. But what I really want to do is work with you directly. You must have more info on the first two girls who vanished than you're telling us."

Lt. Black gave her a close look. "What makes you think that?"

"Because you told us next to nothing. I would like to talk to the families of the missing girls."

"That's out of the question unless I check to see if they want to talk to you. But I can do that tomorrow for you."

"Why not tonight?" she asked.

He started to climb in his car. "I'll see what I can do. I have your number. I'll call you."

"Thanks."

He closed his car door and rolled down his window. "And, Sheila?"

"Yes."

"Watch out who you confide in about this matter. It may be the wrong person."

"I'll remember that," she promised.

5

Dusty Shame sat in his car down the street from Wendy Bart's house and contemplated dark deeds. It was true the house was at the end of a cul-de-sac, as Nancy's had been, but this section of town was even better lit than Chino. A hundred yards behind him was a relatively well traveled road. He found himself reluctant to pull into her driveway, while she was still alive. He was going to break from his pattern, he decided, go inside, kill her, and then walk back for the car. Even though such a change in plan would mean he would be visible longer, he felt it was better to have his car in the Bart driveway for a shorter time. In reality, he was very tense. It was one in the morning, the lights in the house were off, but he didn't know exactly when the parents might return. What if they came in while he was in the house? He would have to kill them all. In light of that possibility he had a switchblade with him, as well as his hammer.

"Help me with this one," Dusty whispered as he quietly got out of his car. He didn't stop to wonder to whom his prayer was directed.

He walked toward the house, feeling haunted. He hoped when he was done with the job, he'd be able to rest. At the beach the sea gulls had circled above him, cackling like hungry vultures, and he had left the ocean with a splitting headache. He hoped Wendy died peacefully.

The Barts had a high wire fence that was a pain to get over. In fact, Dusty got momentarily caught on the jagged wires at the top and suffered the momentary terror of being stuck there when the Barts pulled into their driveway. But he managed to extricate himself, tearing his blue jeans in the process. It was hard to work with gloves on.

He found the back door unlocked.

Wendy loved to be scared—so she thought. Of course that was easy in safe surroundings, to curl up with a book beside a warm fire. The thing was, in the big city no place was safe. Dusty opened the door and walked in.

The Bart home was a one-story ranch. The time he had studied it with his binoculars, he had developed a reasonable idea of where Wendy's bedroom must be—at the far end. But it was only an educated guess.

If the street was annoyingly bright, the house was painfully dark. He walked five feet and kicked something—sounded like a cat food bowl—sending it sloshing over the linoleum floor. He wished he could turn on the light, but knew that would be madness. The cat might take one look at him and try to scratch his eyes out. He couldn't get his nightmare of sightless Nancy out of his mind. What did you do with my eyes? Where did you put my eyes? I want my eyes!

He groped his way down a long dark hallway. There was faint snoring at the end of the hall, and it drew him on. For some reason he had not imagined Wendy as a snorer. He usually had good instincts about things like that. He had pegged Stacy as a snorer just by the way she signed her Led Zeppelin notes on the *Einstein* billboards. The noise was working to his advantage. If Wendy's room was as dark as the hall, he'd just have to aim three inches above the source of the noise and he would hit his target. Snap, crackle, pop—goodbye Miss Gray Matter. Sorry to squash you so late at night, but a man's got to do what he's got to do if he wants to get some decent Zs. Stumbling around in the dark, Dusty wondered why he had never tried sleeping pills. Like a whole bottle at once.

He reached the door beyond which the bellows blew. There he paused to pull out his towel and hammer. The house was insufferably hot and stuffy and his sweat soaked through his gloves to the handle of his weapon, making it slippery to hold. He didn't trust the look of the doorknob because, actually, he couldn't see it. He couldn't tell if it was the kind that sprang halfway to the wall when it was given a little nudge. He had to be careful, he always had to be. They couldn't lock him up until he got to number six. He didn't really care what happened after that. Maybe he'd just blow his brains out, save the taxpayers a few bucks. God, why had Sheila brought Nancy up during chemistry lab?

For some reason, he suddenly wondered where Sheila was at that very moment, what she was doing. He wondered if she was already looking for Nancy, and hoped she wasn't. He liked Sheila, he really did. He liked them all.

Dusty opened the door carefully. The figure on the bed didn't stir, just continued to snore. The room was dark. He crossed to the bed in three long strides. This time, unlike the night before, he didn't pause over the bed. He swooped down over the girl with his towel and at the same time raised his hammer. For an instant her snoring stopped as she inhaled the towel. Then he brought his hammer down hard. The metal cracked the bone cleanly, making a splintering sound that only a fatal blow could. Wendy went limp on the bed.

At peace.

No, he thought, just dead.

Was there a difference?

The room suddenly exploded in light.

Half blinded, Dusty whirled around.

A sleepy-eyed girl stood in the doorway in her nightgown.

"Jenny?" she began, her hand on the light switch.

Dusty leaped. This was Wendy, and she was screaming.

He collided with her and they both went down. He dropped his hammer and couldn't find his switchblade. The light still stung his eyes, and Wendy was one big, strong girl. They rolled on the floor and Wendy landed a rain of blows on his chest, screaming, before he could even get his bearings. The noise she was making worried him more than any harm she was causing him. He shot out his right hand, his glove falling off, and clamped it over her mouth, trying to move into position where he could press her flat to the floor with his knees. He figured he'd cut her throat.

It was a good plan until she bit him.

It was not a little bite.

"Ouch!" he yelled. Now he was calling the neighbors. Blood gushed from his hand. The pain was intense—it brought stars to his eyes. Wendy used the distraction to squirm out from under him and climb to her knees. Before he could recover she was on her feet and running down the hallway toward the kitchen and the cat bowl. In an instant he realized the danger he was in. If she got outside and kept screaming, the neighbors would pour into the street and he would be apprehended. Willing away the pain, he jumped up, grabbed his glove, and chased after her, slipping the glove on to catch the blood.

He caught up to her in the living room—she had not opted for the kitchen, after all—with her hand on the front door. He stopped her dead in her tracks in the living room, but not with his hammer or knife. She was still too far away from him for either of those. He stopped her by calling to her.

"Wendy," he said as he stumbled against the living room wall. The room was wide, she had him beat by more than twenty feet. She had the door partially open; she could be outside on the street in two seconds. But his saying her name made her pause, brought a turn of her head. He realized that, even though they had wrestled, she had not seen him kill whoever it was he had killed. He added hastily, "It's me, William Wand."

She frowned—he saw the expression in a shaft of pale street light that slid in through the cracked door. "Will?" she mumbled.

"Yeah," he said, taking a step toward her. "I took you at your word. I thought you wanted me to come over."

She remained frozen. "Is it really you?"

"Who else but William Wand knows about the bogeyman?" he asked, moving steadily closer, reaching with his left hand for the knife in his back pocket. The cool metal, so reassuring compared to the burning blood that dripped slowly out of his soaked right glove. He was leaving behind a sticky trail on the hardwood floors. Wendy's frown remained, yet a smile touched the corners of it. She probably smiled when she read the scary parts of Mr. King's and Mr. Straub's novels, he thought. She should have been the one who snored.

"Why did you sneak into my house without calling?" she asked, closing the front door.

"You know the answer to that," he said, moving to within five feet of her, fully withdrawing the switchblade from his back pocket, but keeping it hidden from her. He flashed her a winning Dusty Shame smile. She smiled in return.

"Because you wanted to scare me?" she asked, excited.

"Yeah, Wendy." He stepped directly in front of her, at the same time pressing the button on his switchblade. The blade snapped out. He swung the knife around in a single fluid arc. The blade caught her under her rib cage, stabbing through the cotton material of her nightgown with hardly a pause before slicing into her soft flesh. He pulled up hard, steering the razor-sharp point in the direction of her heart. And he must have reached it because Wendy's eyes suddenly went dark just as they had begun to light up. Blood trickled from the side of her mouth. She sagged in his arms and he caught her before she fell. He owed her that much. When she was fully dead in his arms, he brushed back her blond hair and tenderly closed her eyes.

"Because I know you love to be scared," he whispered.

Dusty sat in his car two blocks down the street from Wendy's house and watched through binoculars as her parents' car pulled into the driveway. Mr. and Mrs. Bart climbed out and walked to the front porch. A half hour had elapsed since he had killed the two girls. He didn't know who the other one was, other than *Jenny*—probably some friend who was keeping Wendy company for the night. He had checked to make sure she was dead before he left, though. But he had made no attempt to get the bodies into his car. He felt sure Wendy's screams—and his own—could bring the neighbors, so he had hurried out the back door.

But no one had come running.

That was L.A. for you, Dusty thought in disgust.

He had left his signature card, though.

The voice would never have forgiven him if he had forgotten that.

Now the lights were going on all over the Bart house, and even at this distance he could hear the wails of Wendy's father and mother. He knew that it was foolish to stay, that the police would be there in minutes, but something held him in place. He had never directly witnessed the effect his acts had on families. He had not wanted to see. He had preferred to think of the girls he killed as just numbers to satisfy the mysterious desires of the voice. He watched through his binoculars as the shaken father appeared on the front porch and vomited into the bushes. Puncturing Wendy's heart had spilled more blood than he would have thought possible.

There was blood in his car now as well, although he was being careful. He had wrapped his hand in a strip torn from his shirt. The pain from it was unbelievable. Wendy's teeth had gone deep and hard. He needed medical attention but didn't dare go to a hospital. The police would alert every hospital in the area when they saw the red trail leading to where he had slain Wendy. Plus now the police would have his blood type. It had not been a good night.

Yet he had killed two girls.

Two plus three equaled five.

One more might be all he needed.

Then he could rest.

But not now. He couldn't stop staring at the father through the binoculars. The man's face appeared so close it was as if Dusty could reach out and touch him. But if he did, what would he say to him? Sorry I cut up the light of your life? Mr. Bart would not care how sorry he was. He would just want to kill him. Dusty could see the tears on the man's pale face. A river of tears would follow this night, Dusty realized, and the sorrow of it weighed on his soul like a stone. With tears in his own eyes, Dusty set aside the binoculars and started his car. He could hear sirens approaching. He could not let the authorities catch him, at least not yet.

He had to get something to stop the bleeding, even if there was an element of risk in entering a store. There was a 7-Eleven not far from the freeway and he pulled in there. The place was crowded; it was a happening Friday night and people needed their beer and booze to keep up the joy factor. He kept his right hand in his coat, and since he didn't pull out a gun when he went up to the counter with his two rolls of gauze, medical tape, rubbing alcohol, Coke, and Tylenol, they didn't give him a second look. Back in his car, he swallowed six of the pills with a gulp of soda before he turned to his hand.

A close examination showed him that it was worse than he had thought. A chunk of meat had literally been ripped out of him. He had to have nerve damage as well as torn muscles. The sight of his mangled flesh made him nauseated. He was screwed, he thought, really screwed. Everyone was going to ask what had happened to his hand. He needed stitches in the worst way. For God's sake, he would have thought Wendy was a regular cannibal in her spare time.

Still, he would not go to the hospital.

He opened the bottle of rubbing alcohol with his left hand.

He could not risk infection.

This was going to hurt, he knew.

He gritted his teeth, willing himself not to scream.

He tilted the bottle and poured the liquid over the bloody meat.

Liquid lava. Pain beyond pain.

He passed out, maybe for only a few seconds.

When he came to, he sat up and gave it another splash.

"Mother," he cried. Where was his mother? How come she wasn't there to help him at a time like this? Surely his mother's mother had been there for her. But about his grandmother he knew nothing except that she was dead.

Dusty swallowed another four Tylenol and bent over the passenger seat and screamed into the upholstery. He couldn't catch his breath, the pain wouldn't let him. He sat back up for the second time, his face soaked with tears and sweat. People in the parking lot were beginning to stare at him. He started the car and drove around the block. After parking he rolled down the window and threw up on the street. Shaking badly, he reached for the rolls of gauze. Once he had it covered, he thought, maybe it wouldn't feel so bad.

Twenty minutes later he had his bandage in place. About the same time the Tylenol began to kick in and the pain, although still ferocious, receded somewhat. He sat for a long time taking long, deep breaths. He could hear more police sirens coming from the direction of Wendy's house and suspected half the L.A.P.D. was looking for him. Then again, they didn't know who *him* was.

He felt truly miserable. There was his pain, the image of Wendy's crying father, and Wendy herself, her trusting smile when he told her about the bogeyman. More than any of the others, he had wanted her to go peacefully, without pain or mess. He didn't blame her at all for what she had done to his hand. That would have been unconscionable in his mind. All was fair in love and death.

He didn't want to go home.

He didn't want to go to the cave, not without a body to bury.

He didn't want to go to the *other* place, either.

That horrible place.

But just the thought of it, the memory, was enough to draw him to it. He had been there only once, not long after he had begun to hear the voice. It was, in fact, the voice that had directed him to its location. Although he never heard the voice there, he sometimes imagined the place was the source of the voice. The *tone* of it was there, the feel, like the tension that came in a nightmare that one felt would never end. In that place shadows hung in the air even in the midday sun, black coats belonging to ghosts that still hungered for a taste of living blood. No, Dusty did not like that place.

Yet, after he started his car, he drove there once more.

It was in the foothills of the San Fernando Valley, below the mountains but above the city, at the edge of an old cemetery where the lawns had become tall weeds and ugly trees and bushes. Yet he reminded himself as he drove into the hills that *it* was not actually in the cemetery. Whatever had been buried there, he realized, had been considered too disgusting to lay to rest beside decent people.

"Why am I doing this?" he whispered to himself as he parked his car at the end of a dirt road that led almost up to the cemetery. The stone wall that was supposed to shelter the grave sites from passersby was now piles of rocks that were slowly journeying back to where they had been found. The cemetery had been built before the war, he thought, sure in the knowledge, even though he didn't know which war. Yet coming to this place always made him think of war and battles. He was not completely ignorant of the past. He knew the source of the symbol he left at the scene of each crime.

He got out of his car and walked into the tangle of weeds and grass that was the cemetery. There were no houses in the area. Had there been, the people in them would not have allowed such an outrage of indifference to the dearly departed. But the lack of care didn't bother him. When he died he wouldn't care if he was buried in such a place. Even the cave in the desert would not have bothered him. Because he honestly believed he was one of those rare souls that had no afterlife waiting for him, good or bad. He would just be something rotting in the ground, and the voice would finally be silent.

A ragtag collection of olive and elm and spruce trees led up into the hills away from the cemetery. Here he found another tumbledown wall, but had no trouble scaling it. There was a moon; he could see where he was going without a flashlight, even though he had never been there at night before. The last time had been in the middle of the day, and even then the spot had gotten to him. Now he knew its evil would seep into his soul.

He found the place a minute later.

It was a grave—no question of that, although there was no tombstone. The pile of rocks was arranged in a six foot by three foot rectangle and could only outline one thing. Besides the atmosphere of the spot, the literal horror of what lay under the ground was as palpable as a touch, as loud as a scream. Yes, he was reminded of Wendy's earlier scream as he sat beside the grave. He was reminded of all the young women he had killed, their lost lives. It was almost as if their souls had been sucked to this place after he had finished with their bodies, to be trapped forever. But he prayed that wasn't so because he felt trapped just sitting there. More than anything, he wanted to get up and walk away. But he couldn't move.

He wondered once more why, in this place of all places, he didn't hear the voice.

"Who were you?" he whispered to the ground. "Who *are* you?"

He thought of his mother then, the vegetable, his flower, and suddenly a memory of happier times flooded his mind. He was a boy of five, they were walking hand in hand along the beach. She was telling him stories, and he was enthralled because his mother was the greatest storyteller in the world. The only thing that marred the memory was that he couldn't remember the story. It was sad that he couldn't remember a single thing she had told him. It was as if she had never really existed.

Dusty bowed his head and wept.

6

Saturday morning Sheila Hardholt woke early after a restless sleep. For a moment, just before she was fully conscious, she felt an odd pain, as if something was wrong and she didn't know what it was. But then, when wakefulness hit, she remembered missing Nancy and missing Matt, and the pain went up a hundredfold. It struck her that her waking was the reverse of coming out of a nightmare. Waking should have brought relief, but it only brought agony.

And guilt. Not because she felt in any way responsible for Nancy's disappearance. But because she couldn't stop thinking about Matt when her best friend Nancy might be dead. Matt was her first love, it was true, but if she thought reasonably she knew she would love another, sometime. But if Nancy were gone, she was gone. There would be no other time for her dear friend. God, and they had practically grown up together. Sheila felt Nancy's welfare should take first priority in her heart. Yet she felt equally bad about both Nancy and Matt, hence the source of her guilt. She just wished that during this hard time she could turn to Matt for support. But just seeing him made her feel like a leaf blown this way and that by cruel winds. She knew she had to get a grip before she lost her mind, but she just didn't know what to grab on to.

She didn't want to talk to her parents, though. That, too, was odd. She had always considered herself close to them, able to discuss her deepest feelings openly with both. But when Matt had dumped her, and she had gone crying to them, they had just said he wasn't worth worrying about, and she'd get over it. Yeah, when would she get over it? In two years? She was hurt now, she needed their support now. Yet she did not hold their insensitivity against them. Because they had met and married at an early age, she realized they had never gone through a full-fledged loss. They couldn't relate to her pain.

She couldn't relate to it. She just wished it would go away and leave her in peace. Yet she was terrified to let it go. Because if she did, then she would be giving up all hope that Matt and she would be together again—some day. She didn't want to lose that hope even though she knew it was killing her.

She hadn't told her parents that she sometimes felt like dying.

She hadn't told them she feared Nancy was dead.

Sheila got out of bed at nine o'clock, padded into the kitchen, and ate a bowl of cereal that tasted like paper. She smiled at her parents when they asked how she was and told them fine. Then she returned to her room and called the number Lt. Black had said would beep him immediately. She left a message saying she needed to talk to him, along with her number. When an hour went by and he still hadn't returned her call, she got annoyed, especially after his promise the previous day to be there for them.

Unknown to Sheila, Lt. Black was unable to call because he was still at the Barts'. He had, in fact, been one of the first to arrive at the scene and remained there all night, trying to figure out why the monster had changed his tactics and left a bloody mess.

Waiting around and doing nothing had never been Sheila's strength, but she couldn't be bothered calling her classmates in chemistry because she thought that would be a waste. Dressing, she drove to the library and got out the white pages for L.A. and Orange counties. She remembered the other missing girls' names—Stacy Domino and Debra Weston. Unfortunately there were numerous Dominos and Westons in the books. She'd have to call each number, but she was hesitant. What would she say? "Hi, are you the ones who lost your daughter? I lost my best friend the same way, and I'd like to come over and talk about what a drag it is." Well, maybe she could phrase it more delicately. She really had no choice but to call—she couldn't possibly drive to all the houses listed. Also, she didn't want to drop in on people.

She found Stacy's home quickly—on the third try. It was Stacy's father who answered. His voice sounded flat and didn't warm up when she explained how her friend had disappeared the same way as Stacy. But he didn't say no when she asked if it would be all right if she dropped by to ask a few questions. He didn't exactly say yes, either, but she was going. It was her hope to find something that connected the three girls, something the police might have missed.

Before she left the library she worked on finding Debra Weston of Los Angeles County. This one proved harder. She called over fifteen people, and got a few nasty hang-ups before she reached Debra's mother. The woman sounded so sad the moment she came on the line, Sheila knew she had the right number. But the woman said it would be fine if she stopped over. Sheila suspected she needed someone to talk to.

Sheila drove to Huntington Beach first, to Stacy's house. Mr. Domino answered the door, and she was struck by how much he reminded her of Mr. Bardella. Mr. Domino was a walking zombie. She didn't bother to ask if there was a Mrs. Domino, but she suspected not. But he let her in, and even allowed her into Stacy's room. There she found ample evidence of a girl with a burning passion. There were Led Zeppelin posters everywhere, above Stacy's desktop computer, in her closet, even beside the toilet in her bathroom. Stacy also had an electric guitar and a powerful amp and speakers. Mr. Domino smiled sadly when she asked about Stacy's devotion to the group.

"She could play their CDs ten hours a day," he said. He gestured to the computer. "She was the head of a Led Zeppelin club on one of the computer lines. I never did understand her obsession since the group was popular when I was high school, but she said there was nobody heavier than Zeppelin." He shook his head. "But she was a horrible guitar player herself."

That was the most she got out of Mr. Domino. He wasn't in the mood to talk, and she felt guilty for having bothered him. He let her look around Stacy's room as much as she wanted while he went back to a book in the living room, but she discovered nothing noteworthy, certainly nothing that reminded her of Nancy. Fifteen minutes after arriving at the house, she left.

Debra Weston had lived in San Pedro. On the way there, Sheila stopped and called Matt. He wasn't in, but she got his mother, who sounded annoyed to hear from her. Matt's mother had never liked her. The woman was probably glad, Sheila thought, the two of them had broken up. No, Mrs. Jaye said curtly, she didn't know where Matt was and she didn't know when he would be back. Sheila thanked her for her precious time.

Mrs. Weston lived in a tiny rundown place near the L.A. harbor. She was older; Sheila thought at first she was dealing with Debra's grandmother, not her mother, and made a tactless comment to that effect. But Mrs. Weston must have had Debra late in life. There didn't appear to be a Mr. Weston and Sheila wondered about couples in America and what was happening to them.

Mrs. Weston seemed happy to see her, to share with someone, anyone, a mutual grief. She told how she had been away for the weekend, and how when she came home she found Debra gone and the card with the swastika lying on the bed. It wasn't a long or complicated story. Then the woman burst out crying and Sheila cried with her.

"And she's been gone," Mrs. Weston said, weeping. "And she hasn't come back. And I don't know if she's dead, or if she's hurt, or where she is. And I can't get over it because she was all I have, and I'm afraid I'll never know what happened to her."

Sheila got up and sat beside the woman on a small cheap sofa and put her arm around her. After some time the woman wanted to hear about Nancy, and Sheila told her what she knew, which was little. Then they cried some more and Sheila seriously wondered why she was doing this. Sharing grief did not make it any less, and none of these people had any clues to share. If they had, Lt. Black would have discovered them. Yet Sheila had come there for a purpose, and she felt obligated to ask a few questions. Her first one, of course, was whether Debra was a Led Zeppelin fan.

"Who are they?" Mrs. Weston asked.

"They were a rock group that was popular in the seventies. In fact, they're still popular. They wrote the hit song 'Stairway to Heaven.' Stacy, the first girl who disappeared, was a big fan of theirs. She had started a fan club. I was wondering if there was a connection."

Mrs. Weston shook her head. "Debra didn't listen to much music. She was more into books and movies." She smiled faintly and bit her lower lip. "And boys. Did I tell you she had a boyfriend? His name was Tim. He still calls me every couple of days. He misses her terribly." She sighed. "But I never have anything new to tell him. Lieutenant Black says he has found out nothing."

"I met Black yesterday."

"Such a kind man."

"Yeah," Sheila said. "Would it be possible, Mrs. Weston, to see Debra's room? You understand I'm looking for anything that might connect Debra to Nancy and to Stacy."

Mrs. Weston stood. "I haven't been in her room but once or twice since she left. Too many memories. But Debra always kept it clean. She was a neat girl, and I'm not just saying that because she belonged to me." Mrs. Weston suddenly stopped herself, practically choking. "Lord, I'm talking about her in the past tense."

Sheila put her hand on the woman's shaking arm. "She sounds like a wonderful person. I want to meet her some day. Some day you'll get to meet Nancy, then we'll all get together and have lunch."

Mrs. Weston nodded weakly. "That would be wonderful."

Debra's room was tiny, like the rest of the house, and as Mrs. Weston said, very neat. Yet its sparseness made Sheila's heart sink because there was nothing to study for clues.

Except for one thing.

Debra had a personal computer on her desk.

Sheila stepped over to it. "Does Debra have a modem with this computer?"

"What's that, dear?"

"It's a device that allows a computer to communicate with other computers over the telephone lines."

"Oh, yes. Debra joined a computer club called *Einstein.* It cost fifteen dollars a month to belong to, but it brought her such pleasure I couldn't bear to take it away from her, even though we are always short of money." Mrs. Weston paused. "Did Stacy and Nancy belong to *Einstein?"*

"I know Nancy didn't."

"Oh."

"But Stacy might have. Maybe that's how she formed her club. Mrs. Weston, may I use your phone to call Stacy's father? I can charge the call to my calling card."

Mrs. Weston waved her hand. "Use the phone. Don't worry about the cost."

Sheila used the phone in the living room. Mr. Domino answered after ten rings. He sounded half asleep. He didn't understand Sheila's question at first. Then he explained that he thought Stacy had belonged to a computer club, but he couldn't remember the name of it because Stacy had had a job and took care of her own bills.

"Could you please check her bills?" Sheila asked. "This might be important."

Mr. Domino agreed. He asked if she could call back in ten minutes. While Sheila waited, Mrs. Weston put on tea and told her about the time Debra won the election for treasurer of the student government at her school. Sheila could hardly listen to the woman's reminiscences without wanting to moan. She wished Matt had been home and wondered where he was, who he was with.

Finally she called Mr. Domino back.

Stacy had belonged to *Einstein.*

"When Lieutenant Black spoke to you, did he ask about the computer club?" Sheila asked, excited.

"I'm not sure," Mr. Domino said. "Did any of the others belong to this club?"

"One."

"Oh."

"Look, I'll talk to the lieutenant and check this out. I'll have him call you if it comes to anything."

"It doesn't matter," Mr. Domino said flatly.

"Pardon?"

"She's dead, I know. She's been gone too long to be alive. I don't care if they find out who did it or not. She'll still be dead."

Sheila didn't know how to respond to that. "You take care of yourself, Mr. Domino." She set the phone down. Mrs. Weston was staring at her with dazed eyes. "Stacy belonged to *Einstein,*" she said.

The woman seemed both interested and confused. "But you said Nancy didn't?"

"That's true. Did Lieutenant Black ask you about the computer club?"

Mrs. Weston frowned. "No. But I do remember he asked me about the rock group. I don't know how I forgot that."

"But when you said no about Led Zeppelin, he wasn't interested in the computer club?"

"He never asked about the computer at all," Mrs. Weston said.

Sheila hastily excused herself. She was bursting to talk to Lt. Black. On the road, she pulled over to a phone booth and dialed the number Lt. Black said would have him paged. She got his voice mail and left a message that he was to call her at the phone booth immediately.

He called back in five minutes.

"I've been trying to reach you," Sheila complained.

He sounded exhausted. "I've been preoccupied."

She didn't like the sound of that. "Has another girl disappeared?"

He sighed. "Two girls were murdered in Pasadena last night. Their bodies were not removed from the scene of the crime, but the swastika card was left behind."

Sheila felt faint. "Oh God," she whispered.

"It doesn't mean the others are not alive," he said hastily.

"Of course it does!" she cried into the phone.

"Sheila."

Sheila wept. "If this guy killed these girls, he killed Nancy. Don't try to spoon-feed me hope, Lieutenant. My hope just died." She closed her eyes and leaned against the phone booth. All those fun times she had shared with Nancy—eating pizza late at night, buying clothes together, talking about boys—they were gone. It didn't seem possible. "God," she moaned. "God."

"Sheila, it isn't over till it's over."

Sheila's grief was bitter. "I've had a lot of endings lately. I know what they feel like. My boyfriend's dumping me, did I tell you that? It's over between us and I keep trying to pretend it's not. Well, I'm an idiot, and I'm tired of being an idiot. You're a professional, what do you think Nancy's chances are? Tell me the truth."

He was silent for a moment. "Poor."

"Poor?"

"Extremely poor." He added, "I am sorry."

Sheila nodded to herself. It was better this way. Just leave Nancy to rest, grieve, and get on with life. She had to do the same with Matt. Their chances were extremely poor.

"Did these girls have a computer in their house?" Sheila asked.

"Yeah, I believe so."

"Did they belong to the computer club *Einstein?"*

"I wouldn't know. Why do you ask?"

"Stacy Domino and Debra Weston did."

"How do you know?"

"I was just at their houses. Look, I couldn't wait for your permission. I had to do something, you know?"

"I understand." He considered. "Did Nancy belong to *Einstein?"*

"No," she said reluctantly.

"Then you don't have much of a link. I understand the club is popular."

"Could you just check to see if these latest victims belonged to the club? Then we can argue about how strong the link is."

"I can check right now if you want to hold on," Lt. Black said.

"Sure." She had nowhere to go.

Lt. Black was off the line for five minutes. When he returned, excitement sounded in his voice. "The Barts subscribed to *Einstein,"* he said. "This is quite a coincidence. It's possible the murderer is using the club to find out about his victims, when they'll be alone and the like." He paused. "But what about Nancy?"

Yes, Sheila thought, what about Nancy. This latest news would destroy her parents.

"I don't know," Sheila said. "But maybe we can figure it out if we get together."

"I wouldn't mind talking to you further. I don't know much about how *Einstein* works. Do you?"

"I know a bit about it," she lied.

"I'm in the office right now, but I'll be done here in an hour. I should be home in two. I haven't slept in a couple of days. But I'll wait up for you if you want to stop by. I feel I owe you one, Sheila, for pointing this out to us."

"I'll owe you one if you catch this guy." She didn't feel like Mr. Domino. She wanted the creep's head on a stake. She reached for a piece of paper and a pen in her purse. "Give me your address. I want to come over."

She was off the line and back in her car a minute later. She had a couple of hours to kill, which was no fun when she was carrying around a broken heart in her chest. She knew Lt. Black would quiz her about the computer club, and she wanted to know more about it herself. She supposed she could return to the library and read about it. But then she remembered that Dusty Shame belonged to *Einstein*. He had told her about it one day during chemistry lab. He said it was wonderful. He could probably tell her more about the club in ten minutes than she could learn from a day of study.

Maybe Dusty should go with me to see Lt. Black, she thought.

She decided to drive to Dusty's house first.

7

Dusty Shame was chewing Tylenol and scanning the *Einstein* billboards for a final victim when Sheila Hardholt knocked at his front door. If Sheila believed she had had a bad night, hers was nothing compared to Dusty's. He had found himself unable to leave the cursed grave site until close to sunrise. The place had just said *no,* you will stay by my side, boy, until the rot of my bones seeps into yours. And that was how he felt, as if a filthy spirit had invaded his soul. Then he'd come home, his hand on fire, and lay down only to have the voice come immediately and tell him, endlessly, over and over again, that he had to kill again immediately, that there could be no delay now. Yeah, he told it, I'll do it. Just leave me alone for a few minutes and let me rest. But the voice did not know the meaning of the word *rest.* It knew only pain and death.

He had inserted his wounded hand in a fake cast he had bought in a magic shop—when he had been interested in normal things. He had also made a sling. In many ways a broken arm would be easier to explain than a chewed-up hand, he thought. Also, the cast did protect his wound from getting banged up. He was paranoid everyone was going to connect his injury to Wendy Bart's sharp teeth.

He got up quickly when he heard the knock. His mother and Mrs. Garcia never answered the door. Indeed, no one ever came to visit. For a few agonizing seconds, he wondered if it was the police. But then he saw through the peephole that it was just Sheila, wonderful Sheila. She didn't look so hot. He figured it had something to do with the fact that he had murdered her best friend. He felt kind of bad about that, but at the same time wondered if Sheila might not make a good number six. He didn't really want to kill her, though, since she was a good friend.

"Sheila," he said, opening the door and smiling. "What a wonderful surprise. I didn't know you knew where I lived."

"You told me once approximately where you lived. I found your exact address in the book." She gestured to his sling and cast. "What happened to you?"

"I fell off a hammer—I mean, a ladder."

"Did you break it?"

"Yeah. The doctor says I broke it bad."

"You poor dear. Are you in a lot of pain?"

He shrugged. "Pain's relative, you know. It's a lot when you're the one who has it."

"Ain't that the truth. Hey, can I come in? I have to talk to you about a couple of things."

"Sure." He took an awkward step backward and gestured for her to have a seat on the living room couch. The place was orderly—Mrs. Garcia kept things nice—but he worried that Sheila would pick up on the bad vibes and get suspicious. He figured he was giving off enough weird vibes to give Satan anxiety. "Don't mind the mess," he said.

"There is no mess." She sat on the sofa.

"I was referring to myself," he replied, sitting on a chair across from her. "What can I do for you, Sheila?"

She looked so unhappy right then, it broke his heart. "Things are not good, Dusty. Nancy's disappeared. The police say she's been kidnapped but it looks like she might be dead."

Dusty swallowed. "That's terrible. When did this happen?"

"Thursday night."

"I remember you were worried about her Friday in class. God, are the police sure about this? Maybe Nancy just ran away."

Sheila shook her head miserably. "There's a pattern to these abductions. I can't go into all the details right now. The police asked me not to. But there is something that does seem to connect several of the cases."

"Yeah?" he asked, interested to know what it was.

"It's this computer club you once told me about

—*Einstein.* Remember you told me you belonged to it?"

Dusty gagged. He didn't remember telling Sheila he was a member of *Einstein.* It must have been when he first subscribed to it, before he started killing its members. God, what a blunder.

"Are you all right?" Sheila asked.

"Yeah, I'm fine." He coughed. "I know the club. What do you want to know about it?"

"Well, what I really want you to do is talk to Lieutenant Black. He's in charge of Nancy's case."

"You want me to talk to a cop?"

"Yeah. He wants to learn about the club. I'm supposed to see him in about an hour. I'm going to his house. I was wondering if you could come with me?"

Dusty had to take a moment to have a nervous breakdown. So the police were onto where he got his victims. That meant they would soon be investigating William Wand, and eventually end up at his post office box. That wasn't a catastrophe because he had secured it with a phony ID. On the other hand, the post office box was local, just a mile from his house, and they would know they were dealing with someone in the neighborhood, possibly someone who had known Nancy personally. For sure, he could not use *Einstein* to find any more innocent young things to practice his carpentry on.

But Sheila was making him an interesting offer. If he spoke to this Lt. Black directly he might learn what the police knew and didn't know. He might learn something that could save his ass. Of course, there was always the possibility that Lt. Black would arrest him on the spot. The cop must know that Wendy Bart had wounded her assailant before she had embraced the knife, and here he was missing a part of his hand. For all he knew, the cops might have a description of him.

Yet Dusty decided the possible payoff was worth the risk. He was just a teenager who had broken his arm. High school kids were always breaking things. Lt. Black wouldn't suspect him unless he made another remark about his hammer. That sure had been a cute little Freudian slip.

"If you don't want to go because your arm hurts too much, I'll understand," Sheila said, watching him. He was taking too long to respond.

"No, no, I'll go. If I can help Nancy in any way, I have to go." He stood. "Let me wash up a second and I'll be right out."

"You're such a dear," Sheila said.

He squeezed her shoulder as he walked by. Such a dear.

In his bedroom he quickly turned off his computer and disposed of all the notes he had collected on *Einstein* murder candidates. He tore them into tiny shreds, wishing he had a real shredder like the bigwigs in Washington D.C. He thought of tearing up his last swastika card but decided he might need it before he could make another one. He was going to have to do a lot of things soon with this Lt. Black character breathing down his neck.

When he returned to the living room, he discovered his mother had wandered out from her bedroom and was standing in the center of the living room—in her bathrobe, of course—staring at Sheila. His poor lab partner was staring back; it was obvious she didn't know what to do. Dusty moved hastily to his mom's side, just as Mrs. Garcia popped out of her bedroom.

"Sheila, this is my mom," Dusty said, taking his mom's right arm. "I told you she's not herself these days. This other woman is Mrs. Garcia, our helper."

"Hi, Mrs. Shame," Sheila said, smiling. "Pleased to meet you. I'm good friends with your son. Hi, Mrs. Garcia."

"Hi," Mrs. Garcia said nervously, glancing from Sheila to Dusty.

What class, Dusty thought, to address his mother as if she were a normal person when she obviously didn't have a functional brain cell left in her skull. He really mustn't kill Sheila, he decided, not unless he absolutely had to. With Mrs. Garcia's help, he steered his mother back toward her bedroom.

Then something remarkable happened.

His mother suddenly shook off his hand and pointed her arm at Sheila. She even extended her index finger, till it was aimed directly between Sheila's eyes.

"Ahhhh," her mother moaned, saliva dripping from the side of her open mouth. Stunned, Dusty watched for a moment before doing anything. His mother hadn't raised an arm in over five years. Now three times in a couple of days.

"I'm sorry about this," Dusty said finally, taking hold of his mother once more. Her arm came down easily, but he could not erase the memory of a few seconds ago, the way she had shaken him off, the strength in her. She had almost scared him, his own mother. He steered her toward her bedroom with his good hand. "I'll be back in a minute," he told Sheila.

"Take your time," she said, obviously spooked.

8

Lt. Black lived in the Westwood area, not far from U.C.L.A. His house was small, but attractive: red bricks, manicured lawn, white picket fence, fat Persian cat curled up on the front porch. Dusty Shame checked out the place in case he had to break into it later. It had become a reflex with him.

A pretty blond-haired girl, approximately fourteen years old, greeted them at the door. Her silvery blue eyes were practically the same color as her braces, her shorts smaller than her daddy would have liked. She had a glow about her, Dusty thought, the way Sheila had before Matt and Nancy had begun to torture her.

"Hi, are you Sheila?" the girl asked.

"Yes," Sheila said. "We've come to see Lieutenant Black. Is he here?"

"Yes. He just jumped in the shower. Please come in. My name's Dixie—I know it's weird. I'm the lieutenant's daughter."

The decor was white, modern, lots of glass. Dusty hated it. He disliked places that easily absorbed the filth he believed he always carried with him. All the furniture in his house was dark, safe. Dixie had them sit on the white couch before disappearing into the kitchen. Sheila looked over at him.

"Does your arm hurt?" she asked.

"No."

"I saw you swallow four aspirin in the car."

"They were Tylenol."

"I shouldn't have forced you to come," Sheila said.

"I belong here."

"What did you think of Dixie?"

"She looks innocent," Dusty said.

Lt. Black appeared a few minutes later, dressed in blue jeans and a gray sweater. His casual dress did nothing to remove his aura of authority, which Dusty immediately sensed and distrusted. Sheila introduced them. Dusty shook with his left hand. They returned to their places on the couch, Lt. Black sitting across from them. Sheila quickly explained why he was there, the supposed expert on the inner workings of the computer network *Einstein*. Lt. Black was interested.

"Is it possible to write to individual people using the network?" he asked.

"Yes, sir," Dusty said. There would be no point in lying to the man. He could, and surely would, check the validity of what he said against another source. "You can E-mail anybody you wish with their ID number, which appears beside their name. It doesn't mean the person will respond, of course."

"What are these clubs?" Lt. Black asked.

"They're in the bulletin board section, which is divided into sections—art, movies, music, books, so on. Under music there might be a place to talk about the rock group U2. You can write notes or you can respond to other people's notes. Usually, the bulletin boards are excuses to socialize. But sometimes you find something interesting."

"Interesting?" Lt. Black asked. "How so?"

What was interesting to Dusty was discovering a young female who lived in the area and who was susceptible to bait. But he couldn't say that. He shrugged.

"It depends on your tastes what you might find interesting," Dusty replied. "Sir."

"You don't have to call me sir."

"All right," Dusty said.

"I'm interested in this private E-mail," Lt. Black went on. "Is there any way to find out someone's phone number or address using this type of mail?"

"Only if the person who responds to you gives it to you. The service doesn't list this information. The service strongly discourages people from giving out their phone numbers and addresses."

"But do people do it?" Lt. Black asked.

Dusty hesitated. He had to remind himself that he was safer with the truth; if he lied, Lt. Black might later wonder why. Already, he wished he had not come. The cop had a way of looking at him that made Dusty feel uncomfortable.

"Yes," Dusty said. "All the time."

"Have you done it?" Lt. Black asked.

"No. I don't spend a lot of time on the boards."

"Why not?"

"They bore me."

"But teenagers in general like them?"

"Yes. They're very popular."

"Is there a Led Zeppelin club on the boards?"

"I think there are several," Dusty said.

"What happened to your arm?"

"Pardon?"

"Your arm. You have it in a sling."

"I broke it using a ladder to change a light bulb."

Sheila smiled. "You should have used your fingers, Dusty."

Dusty forced a grin, although he felt like peeing his pants. Lt. Black continued to watch him. But maybe he was just that sort, Dusty thought, always observing.

"I'll remember that next time," Dusty said.

"I'm having *Einstein* set up in my home tomorrow," Lt. Black said. "I would appreciate it if you could come back then and help me find my way around in it?"

Dusty shrugged. "Anything I can do to help."

"Sheila's told you about your missing classmate?"

"Yes. It's very sad."

"I didn't talk about the stuff that you asked me not to talk about," Sheila said hastily.

"Speaking of which, there are a few things I would like to discuss with you in private, Sheila," Lt. Black said. "Would you mind leaving us alone for a few minutes, Dusty? I know I'm being rude but it's police business, and Sheila's sort of turning into a deputy of mine. Perhaps you can wait in the kitchen with Dixie. She's supposed to be baking a cake, but I think it's threatening to become a loaf of bread. She said something about having forgotten to put in the sugar."

Dusty stood. He would pump Sheila later, she would tell him what they talked about. He was not worried now that Lt. Black thought he was a murderer. He would hardly send him to be alone with his daughter.

"I like cake," he mumbled. He made his way in the direction Dixie had disappeared.

She was indeed earnestly at work on some doughy masterpiece. She had her hair pinned up and wore a bright pink apron over her red shorts. He explained that he had been kicked out and asked to wait offstage. She offered him a stool at the counter, which he accepted.

"Dad does that to me a lot," Dixie said. "He'll be on the phone talking to somebody, and then he'll wave his arm and I'll have to leave the room. And sometimes I'm watching TV and it's not fun."

"I'm sure he has many responsibilities."

"Yeah. He's strict but he's pretty cool, too." Her

eyes widened and she picked up a spoon. "You know what he's working on now? Those murder cases where that guy kills teenage girls. Have you heard about it?"

"That's why we're here. One of our friends has disappeared."

"Oh, wow, that's terrible. Like, I would just die if one of my friends died. I hope it wasn't your girlfriend or anything like that."

"I don't have a girlfriend."

Dixie seemed pleasantly surprised. "You don't? How old are you? Are you still in high school?"

"I'm a senior."

"I'm a freshman. I know that sounds pretty uncool, but most of my friends at school are sophomores and juniors. I hang out with them. Most of the freshmen at our school are so immature that I can't relate to them at all. Do you ever have that problem, just relating to people?"

"Sometimes."

Dixie reached for a mixing bowl. "Well, I hope your friend's OK. If anyone can find her, my dad can. He works himself to death. He was out all last night and he's going back to work in a couple of hours and he told me he's not coming back till early morning again. Can you believe that?"

"You and your mother must get lonely for him."

Dixie made a face. "Oh, my mom, she split when I started talking. There are just the two of us here."

"That's a shame," Dusty Shame said.

* * *

"I should be mad at you," Lt. Black said to Sheila as soon as Dusty was out of the room. "You weren't supposed to talk to those people without my permission. Fortunately neither has called to complain."

"I'm sorry," Sheila said.

"But as I said on the phone, I understand. You were behaving like a true friend. You had to try to help Nancy somehow. On the force, I sometimes bend the rules to get things done. Sometimes it seems the only way to get something done is to ignore my superiors." He leaned forward in his chair and rubbed his hands together. Once more Sheila was struck by how handsome he was. Yet she hardly entertained the thought when an image of Matt popped in her mind, and she felt pain surging in her chest. Lt. Black continued, "I'm wondering if it's possible we could lure this killer out by posing on the *Einstein* boards as a young woman who's from this area and often alone?"

"I thought the same thing," Sheila said. "But you might be on the boards a long time before he noticed you. From what Dusty said, it sounds like there are hundreds of clubs."

"We have to start somewhere."

"Did you learn anything new from the murders last night?"

"A few things. We now know the murderer's blood type. We also know he's Caucasian. One of the victims bit her assailant before being killed. We uncovered bits of skin from her mouth."

"I suppose that's helpful," Sheila muttered, feeling sick to her stomach. "Anything else?"

Lt. Black sighed. "This part is particularly unpleasant. One girl was asleep in her bed when she was killed by a blow to the head with a hammer. The second girl, whose house it was, appears to have discovered the killer in the act. They wrestled in the doorway before the girl was able to slip free for a moment. It was during that wrestling match the girl bit him. But he caught up with her in the living room and stabbed her through the heart with a knife."

Sheila felt the blood drain from her face. "Go on."

"A towel had been thrown over the head of the girl in the bed. We believe his use of the hammer and the towel has been his primary mode of operation. He covers the girls then strikes them on the head while trying not to spill any blood. We further believe that he was taken by surprise by the second girl and only used the knife because he had to." He paused. "You see the significance of what I'm saying?"

Sheila nodded weakly. "That he probably covered Nancy with a towel before smashing in her brains."

"It looks like that. We have since found a faint trace of Nancy's blood on her sheet." He paused again. "This is a dirty business, Sheila. I wish you hadn't run up against it while you're still so young."

Sheila's eyes burned. She lowered her head. How many more times was she going to have to bury Nancy? She knew her friend was dead when she had last spoken to Black. Now, though, there could be no doubt.

"Have you told her parents?" Sheila whispered.

"Not yet."

"Maybe I should tell them. I'm close to her mother."

"That might be best. It's difficult to hear news like this from a stranger."

Sheila looked up. "Why didn't he take the bodies this time?"

"There was some noise. Neighbors heard it. The killer probably got scared and fled. But, as I told you, he left his calling card. And that's what I wanted to talk to you about. You were right yesterday when you accused me of withholding information. But I did so because I considered this information dubious at best. I suppose I still do, yet I feel compelled to talk to you about it. I'm not even sure why. Maybe it's because of your uncovering the *Einstein* connection. That was a brilliant stroke of investigative work on your part, Sheila."

"Thank you," she said, although she considered everything she had learned to be too little too late. She wondered what Lt. Black's problem was with the hidden information. He appeared embarrassed to talk about it. He fidgeted on the sofa before he continued.

"I guess I should just blurt this out," he said

finally. "We have on our files a case similar to one that's happening now."

"You're kidding? How similar?"

"It's virtually identical. Young women vanished from their beds in the night, never to be found. A white card with a black swastika was left at the scene of each crime. Six woman all together who were taken."

"This case was never made public?"

"No."

"I'm surprised," Sheila said. "It would have been one of the most famous murder mystery cases in history."

"There were reasons the police at that time wanted to suppress knowledge of the case."

"What were they?"

"I'll get to those in a moment."

"Please, Lieutenant, just tell me what you know. If the case was not made public, then it must be the same person behind these recent attacks."

Lt. Black shook his head. "Hardly. These events occurred in 1945, not long after the end of World War Two."

Sheila frowned. "That was half a century ago. Was the murderer ever caught?"

"We think so."

"You're not sure?" Sheila asked.

"We had an officer on the force at that time named Captain Gossick. He was a celebrated war veteran. He had fought in Europe against the Nazis and had been one of the first men to enter Dachau, the original concentration camp where tens of thousands of Jews were executed. He was a personal friend of General Patton. He saw a lot of action, is what I'm saying, and proved himself under the most trying circumstances. The Los Angeles Police Department was happy to have him."

"Is he the one who killed the girls?" Sheila asked.

Lt. Black was shocked. "Oh, not at all. Captain Gossick was a highly moral individual. He was a hero, as I said. But then these murders started, just like the ones today. Of course, no one knew they were murders at first. The girls were just gone. Gossick was put in charge of the case. He worked on it night and day. He became obsessed with it, it's been said. But he worked alone. The leads he was chasing—his fellow officers thought he was wasting his time. You see, he thought the murders had something to do with the Nazis. Now obviously a card with a swastika was left at the scene of each crime. Any logical person, particularly at that time in history—just after what the world had gone through with Germany—would have thought there was a connection. But Gossick's slant on the matter was unique. He believed the *power* of the Nazis was behind the crimes."

"What do you mean, the *power?*" Sheila asked.

Lt. Black shook his head. "No one knew what Gossick meant, not exactly. He seemed to have this idea that there was an evil force behind what Hitler and his cronies did during the war. And that that same force was at work in the abductions of the girls."

"He believed in the occult?"

"It depends on how you define *occult.* The word literally means 'that which is hidden.' It only developed its unsavory reputation recently, largely because of fanatical religious groups. But, yes, from what I've seen, I would say Gossick believed in the occult. But I would say he definitely saw himself on the good side of unseen forces, as opposed to the bad side. Anyway, let me go on. Six women were taken during the night and never seen again. The abductions only stopped when Gossick shot and killed a woman named Madame Scheimer."

"A woman was behind the murders?" Sheila gasped.

"We think so. But we're not sure. Gossick never arrested the woman. She was never brought to trial. He just shot her and said he had got his man, even though it was a woman. He was kicked off the police force for it. But as I said, the murders did stop."

"Who was this Madame Scheimer?"

"This is where it gets interesting. She was Heinrich Himmler's girlfriend. Do you know who he was?"

"He was the second most powerful man in Nazi Germany. He headed the SS and was in charge of the concentration camps."

"I see you learned your history well. Many have

described Himmler as worse than Hitler. Madame Scheimer is not well known. In fact, only a few historians know of her. After the war she vanished. Until Gossick found her living in Los Angeles and killed her."

"How did he find her?"

"I don't know."

"Did he ever say why he didn't arrest her?"

"Yes. His reason was probably the reason he was kicked off the force. He was lucky he didn't go to jail. He said she was too dangerous to be kept in any human prison, that she would just get out and go on killing."

"But I'm confused," Sheila said. "If Gossick did kill the woman, and she was behind the murders, then how could they start up again in exactly the same manner?"

"The most obvious answer is that he got the wrong person. And that this person is still alive and killing again. But it's not a very good answer because it means we're dealing with a murderer who is old—seventy, at least."

"What do you think?"

"I honestly don't know what to think. The murders did stop with the death of Scheimer. Yet they've restarted again, fifty years later. It makes no sense whatsoever that this could just be a coincidence. I refuse to accept that explanation, but I don't know what to do with what Gossick says."

"He's still alive?" she asked.

"Yes. That's what I've been leading up to. We had the case in our files, and when the abductions started, I sent a couple of men out to talk to Gossick. I was grasping at straws, I know, but sometimes you never know where a straw will lead. My men didn't get much out of him. He lectured them for hours on the evil behind Hitler and Himmler, and also how Madame Scheimer embodied that evil, and how he was not surprised it had resurfaced again. But he gave them nothing substantial to go on. I stopped by to see him myself, although not for long. Since this started, I haven't had a spare minute. I found him to be pretty weird. He's in his eighties, could be a little senile, but at the same time he has a remarkable memory for things that happened a long time. But he was mad at me from the moment we met because apparently my men had not taken him or his warnings seriously. We did not speak long, and I learned nothing of interest. But while I was there, his great-granddaughter came to visit, and I noticed how well he communicated with her, how open he was. But the openness vanished the moment he turned back to me."

Lt. Black paused and studied Sheila for a moment. She had a feeling what he was going to say next. "You want me to talk to him?" she asked.

"Yes."

She had to laugh, although she felt far from merry. "Because I might remind him of his great-granddaughter? I don't know anything about the Nazis. He won't talk to me."

"He'll talk to you if you'll listen to him. That's where I think my men erred. They assumed that because he was old he was a fool. But I don't think Gossick is a fool. He did great things in the war. He was a brilliant detective until he was kicked off the force. He may be old, but he may be quite insightful, too."

"Then you should go talk to him again," Sheila said.

"I don't have the time. You're young but *you* have the necessary skills. You spotted an important connection we all missed."

"I was lucky."

"We could all use some luck right now, Sheila."

She was doubtful. "I can't just show up at his place."

"I called him. He's expecting you this evening at nine o'clock."

"What did you tell him about me?"

"That you lost a friend in this latest sequence of abductions. It was the right approach. He was sympathetic. I told him you just wanted to understand what was happening, and that you had an open mind."

"He wasn't suspicious?" Sheila asked.

"Why would he be? I told him the truth."

"The truth? I didn't know who he was until you just told me."

"That's a technicality. I think you do want to talk to him."

"Why do you say that?"

Lt. Black was shrewd. "Do you want to talk to him?"

She considered. "Yeah. I guess it couldn't hurt. Why can't I go see him now?"

"His kidneys are failing him. He gets dialysis Saturday afternoons, then has to sleep for a few hours afterward. He told me he's usually at his best between nine and twelve at night. Honestly, he seemed happy to have a young visitor. Maybe he's lonely, I don't know. But talk to him. See if you can find out anything about the previous killings to help us now."

"Where does he live?" she asked.

"In Ventura."

"Can I bring Dusty with me?"

"Why do you want to bring him?"

"Ventura is up north, the opposite direction from my house. I'll have to drive Dusty all the way back to my neighborhood if I don't take him."

"I wouldn't bring him."

Sheila was surprised at Lt. Black's reaction. "Why not?"

Lt. Black glanced in the direction of the kitchen. "Dusty seems a nice young man, but there's something about him that drags. I don't think he's a happy person."

"He's had a hard life. His mother is ill."

"That's a shame. But you're very personable,

Sheila. I think you alone will be able to get Gossick to open up."

"Could Matt come? You met him yesterday."

"Your boyfriend?" He stopped. "I'm sorry, you said something about the two of you breaking up?"

Sheila drew in a burning breath. "Yeah, he's dumping me."

"He must be a fool."

She forced a smile. "Could you tell him that?"

"Were you going together long?"

"Yeah."

"It was serious then?"

"I took it seriously."

His manner was gentle. He could see the pain the breakup caused her. A blind man probably could have seen it.

"I would tell him that if it would help," Lt. Black said. "But it won't. My wife left me one day. She was the center of my life. I loved her completely, and I thought she loved me. But then one day I came home from work and she told me she was in love with another man that she had met, that she had been involved with him for six months." He paused. "I wanted to quit then, just check out, get off the planet. But I had Dixie to care for, and I had my responsibilities at work." He cleared his throat. "So I know how you feel, Sheila. The only thing I can tell you—and I know it's not much—is that time will make it better if you give yourself that time."

She sniffed, she was such a sap. She had to stop

bleeding like this in public. It was humiliating. She nodded out of respect for his advice because it was good advice.

"That's what I'm trying to do," she said.

He stood. "Good girl. Let me get you Gossick's address. I'll give you his phone number as well, in case you get lost. Call me after you've spoken to him. Hopefully we'll both have more to tell each other."

"With all that's going on, don't you worry about Dixie?"

He stopped with his foot on the stairway and glanced back at her. "I worry a lot, Sheila. If anything did happen to Dixie, I would die." Then he shrugged. "But it's a big city. I figure the odds of that bastard coming into my home are a million to one."

Sheila blinked, feeling an inexplicable chill. For some reason, the odds he quoted didn't sound right. Maybe Gossick could tell her why.

"Yeah," was all she said.

9

Sheila Hardholt drove Dusty Shame back toward Chino. Along the way they stopped at a McDonald's and had a hamburger and fries. Dusty had trouble eating with his arm in the cast and she had to help him a few times. He was curious about the murders, and asked her a number of questions while they ate. But she was not in the mood to talk and, besides, Lt. Black had asked her to keep the matter confidential. She made no mention whatsoever of Captain Gossick and Madame Scheimer. Dusty was pleasant company, though, and she was glad to have him with her. She wished she wasn't obsessed with Matt and could have gone out with Dusty instead, just for fun.

Dusty's arm must have been hurting worse than he let on. In the car he popped Tylenols like they were candy. She told him that he could overdose on them, but he just laughed off the warning. He said that he knew his limits.

At his house she walked him to the door. The housekeeper, Mrs. Garcia, was sitting on the front porch but quickly got up and went inside as they approached. She flashed Sheila the strangest look before she disappeared—it was almost one of relief. Sheila paid it little heed.

"Thanks for coming," Sheila told Dusty, giving him a quick hug. "You made the long drive each way so much more enjoyable. Thanks for buying me a hamburger, too."

"Our first date and I took you to the best of places," he joked.

"Hey, I'm a single girl now. If you want to take me some place else, I'm available."

His face became sad all of a sudden. "Are you serious?"

She hesitated. She had been joking. No one knew better than she what lousy company she was these days. But she did like Dusty, and wouldn't have minded getting to know him better. Just for fun, she thought again.

She didn't know why her invitation had depressed him so.

"Sure," she said. "I'd love to go out with you." She chuckled and socked him on his good arm. "Don't look so gloomy about the prospect!"

He forced a smile. "It's not that. I just . . ." His voice trailed off and he shrugged.

"It's just what?" she asked gently.

He fidgeted and looked at the ground. "You don't

know me very well, Sheila. I'm not like the other guys at school."

"That's good. It makes you an individual."

He glanced up. "No, it's bad. It just makes me different." He took a deep breath and expelled it on a sigh. He really was struggling with something, Sheila could see. He coughed as a tremor appeared to go through his body. "I have trouble with relationships," he said.

"In relating to girls?"

He nodded. "It's always been hard for me, you know, to be myself around them. No, that's not it. I don't want to be myself around them."

"Why not?"

He shook his head again. "Because I'm not that nice a guy."

She laughed. "Dusty! You are absolutely the sweetest guy I know at school. Look, you just need to get out more and get experience with girls. You'll find they're not the scary creatures you imagine them to be. And if you want to go out with me sometime, I'd be honored. I mean that sincerely."

He blinked in surprise. "I thought you wanted to fix me up with Nancy?"

That quieted her down. Her voice came out soft. "I suppose that won't be possible now, will it?"

"I'm sorry, I shouldn't have said that."

She squeezed his arm. "Hey, you didn't mean anything by it. These are just bad times. Bad times can't last forever. Things have got to get better for all of us."

"Do you believe that?" he asked, genuinely curious.

"I do. I have to believe it." She gave him a quick kiss on the cheek and began to back toward her car. "You take care of yourself. Call me sometime."

His face brightened. "Will you be home later?"

"Not until real late, after eleven or twelve. But you can call me if you want. I have my own phone in my room."

"I wouldn't want to wake you," he said.

"Who cares?" She opened her car door. "You can even stop by if you want. I need a friendly face nowadays more than I need sleep."

Dusty waved goodbye. "I'll think about it," he said.

It was seven in the evening, and the sun was close to the horizon when Sheila pulled out of Dusty's street. Ventura was at least an hour and a half away. She would have to start up north soon, she realized. But the thought of the long drive alone, after having had the pleasure of Dusty's company, weighed heavy on her. Practically everything did. Her chest had turned into a regular scientific scale capable of measuring and recording even a microgram of human suffering. And somebody kept piling on the weight.

She decided to call Matt. What else was there to decide? Lt. Black had not actually said no to her idea of bringing Matt. Plus her ex was as personable as she, maybe more so. Gossick might hit it off with Matt better, she reasoned. Besides if she didn't talk to him soon, she was going to start crying. She pulled over to a phone booth at a gas station near her house. She got his mother again.

"Is Matt there?" Sheila asked.

"Who is this?"

"Sheila."

"I thought you broke up?"

"We did."

"Then why are you calling all the time?"

"Because I still love your son, Mrs. Jaye. I love him more now that we're broken up than ever before. And it's hard for me not to talk to him. And if you had an ounce of feeling inside you, you'd realize that and not grill me every time I call." Sheila paused to catch her breath. "Is Matt there?"

The woman was a while answering. "I'll get him," she said flatly.

Matt was on the line a minute later. "Sheila, what did you say to my mom?"

"Is she upset?"

"That's one way of putting it."

"Well, I'm sorry, I gave her a piece of my mind. She'll get over it in six months. Anyway, things are not looking good for Nancy. Somebody killed two girls in Pasadena last night and left the same calling card."

Matt sounded crushed. "Damn. Do her parents know about this?"

"I don't think so. I don't think it's been on the news yet. Also, even if it has been, the police won't let out the thing about the swastika card."

"Somebody should tell them."

"I'm going to," Sheila said. "But I have to do something first and I want you to do it with me. I have to drive to Ventura to talk to an old cop who had experience with a similar killer fifty years ago."

"Fifty years ago?"

"It's fascinating," She paused. "If you want to come with me I can tell you all about it?"

"Why are you going?"

"Because I'm special, Matt, remember? You used to tell me that."

"Sheila."

"I'm sorry, I shouldn't have said that. Lieutenant Black told me to go, and I want you to come." I need you to come, she thought.

"But you keep telling me that seeing me hurts you."

"I hurt either way. Please come with me. Please, Matt?"

He sounded reluctant. "If you want me to come, I'll come."

He looked so good when she picked him up, and she knew she must look like hell. You could always tell the one who got dumped, she thought, just by their faces. It annoyed her that he seemed so at ease, though. But she did not tell him that. She was just happy when he got in the car beside her.

"You were smart not to come to the door," he said.

She laughed softly. She had always wanted to tell off Mrs. Jaye. The woman had been a pain in the ass since she had first started going out with Matt.

"I guess she won't be coming to the wedding," she said.

"Oh, brother. Tell me about this cop?"

She explained what she knew as she drove. She also described what Lt. Black had said about the murders the night before. Matt shared her opinion —Nancy must be dead.

Yet, on the whole, they didn't talk a lot on the drive to Ventura, not as they had when they were going together. Sheila found it impossible not to discuss their breakup endlessly, and Matt obviously was tired of the subject. So they listened to the radio and watched the scenery go by.

Captain Gossick was sitting on his front porch as they drove up. By then the night was almost complete. Gossick's place was small and homely, the lawn overgrown, the exterior paint peeling. Gossick sat on an old wicker chair with a pipe in his hand, light coming through a screen door from inside the house. He stood as they approached, and Sheila saw that even though he was very old, he appeared fit, his posture straight, his shoulders broad. His grip was firm as he shook both their hands in welcome. His face was shrunken with age, but it was easy to see he had been an imposing man in his youth. He had dark blue eyes that twinkled as he studied them. They introduced themselves.

"You drove all the way from Chino?" he asked, gesturing for them to take a seat on a cramped wicker love seat opposite his chair. They got settled as Gossick once more picked up his pipe. The night air was warm, calm.

"We drove straight through," Sheila said. "It's a nice drive."

"I bet at least one of you has to use the restroom," he said. "You're welcome to."

Sheila blushed. "We stopped at a gas station down the street a few minutes ago."

That made him smile. "Can I offer you some lemonade?" he asked, gesturing to a pitcher and glasses set beside him on a small table. She realized he had prepared it especially for their visit—or hers, at least—and was touched.

"I'd love some," she replied.

"That would be great," Matt agreed.

"I have a lemon tree in the back," Gossick said, his hands trembling as he poured their drinks. "It's the craziest thing. It grows lemons all year. It never pays attention to the seasons."

"It must be a magic tree," Sheila said, accepting her ice-filled glass from him. The lemonade was delicious, very sweet, the way she liked it. "Good," she said.

Gossick was pleased. He poured a glass for himself. "I've been a great believer in the vitamin C in citrus fruits long before it became fashionable.

It's been ten years since I caught a cold or flu. If it wasn't for my damn kidneys, I'd be the picture of health."

"Lieutenant Black said you have to go for dialysis every Saturday?" Sheila asked.

"Three times a week," Gossick corrected her. "I feel like a cyborg in the *Terminator* movies, sitting there with that needle in my arm, hooked up to that blasted machine." He scowled. "I hate that place and the nurses who work there. They all treat me like a patient when they are the ones who need help. The things they gossip about, you'd swear they only taught them how to read the *Enquirer* and do their nails in school."

"I never read the *Enquirer,"* Sheila said.

"I do," Matt added.

Gossick grinned, flashing a set of tobacco-stained dentures. "As long as you don't do your nails, son, we'll get along fine." He reached for a bag of tobacco and began to ready his pipe. "Mind if I smoke?"

"It's your house," Sheila said.

"That's what I told them two young officers," he quipped. "The ones Lieutenant Black sent to talk to me. But they didn't like my smoking, no way. Their eyes got all red and teary. Imagine that, cops who don't smoke." He laughed low, his throat scratchy. "But they were all right." He glanced at Matt. "I didn't expect you, Matt."

"Sheila asked me to come," Matt said.

"Matt was a close friend of Nancy's also," Sheila

said hastily. "That's the name of our friend who disappeared."

Gossick nodded. "I know her name. I still have friends in the department. They keep me abreast." He paused. "I'm sorry about your friend. I suppose you heard about what happened last night?"

Sheila nodded. "Yes. We don't have much hope for Nancy."

Gossick was grim. "I'm glad you feel that way, and I truly hate to say that. But I knew the night your friend was taken that she was dead."

"How?" Matt said.

Gossick took out a wooden match, struck it on the side of the table holding the lemonade, and lit his pipe. "That's the story, isn't it? Do you want to hear it? The other two that came—they wanted 'something concrete to go on,' they told me. But my story isn't made of concrete. It's like my lemon tree, magical. But there are two kinds of magic in this world, black and white. And this story is black."

"We want to hear everything," Sheila said.

Gossick puffed on his pipe and studied her once more. His blue eyes, even with their twinkle, were powerful when focused. Yet they were tender, too, and she didn't feel uneasy to be sitting so close to him. Indeed, she found it a comfort to be with him and didn't understand why. He was bit gruff, yet he seemed at peace. She wished she could be at peace. Gossick seemed to read her mind.

"I do believe you know something of magic, child," he said. "And pain."

"This whole experience has been painful," she said, and she couldn't help but glance at Matt as she spoke. Gossick noticed where her eyes strayed. He nodded once more.

"I'll tell you my story," he said. "But I have to begin more than fifty years ago, with a character who is not the principal character of the tale. But even though I say that, he and she were the same, in their wicked hearts."

"He and she?" Matt asked.

"Reichsführer SS Heinrich Himmler and his personal bitch, Madame Olga Scheimer," Gossick said. "The two worst vessels of corruption this century has seen. My story is about them." He took a puff on his pipe and then began.

"Himmler was strange even as a child. There are stories of his phenomenal memory, how he could recall incredible details of German history, a history he had learned from his father, a professor. Yet though Himmler seemed obsessed with Germany's past greatness, his memory was often described as colorless. What I mean by that is he was like a machine that absorbed facts for the sake of facts, not for what they could teach him.

"Himmler appeared to his schoolmates as a nonentity. He lacked human warmth and personality. But his friends were also afraid of him because he had a reputation as an informer. Even when young, he could turn on a friend and feel nothing. That was to be a trademark of his career.

"When he was of age, he applied to be a professional soldier, but even with his family connections he was turned down because he was found both physically and psychologically unsuitable. This was immediately after the First World War. He was a weedy young man with a high-pitched voice and thick glasses that magnified his eyes. Most people found him repulsive.

"After World War One a man by the name of Adolf Hitler was making his first moves toward power. Hitler had been in jail at the Landsberg Fortress for annoying the government with his new Nazi party, and when he emerged, the first thing he did was form the *Schützstaffel* or Protective Guards—the SS. They were Hitler's personal bodyguards. A close friend of Hitler, George Strasser, hired Himmler to help with the SS, not out respect for Himmler's abilities, but because Himmler knew a thing or two about chemistry, and Strasser had been a chemist before he had joined the Nazi party. This was the first event that linked Himmler to Hitler and started the unlikely chain of events that would lead to Himmler's rise to power.

"Hitler had to find employment for the volunteer members of his newly formed SS and did so by largely taking over the party newspaper, *Der Volkischer Beobachter,* and employing these people as sellers of advertising space. Strasser was put in charge of this operation, and by this time Himmler had become his secretary. At the paper Himmler collected information about the activities of local Communists and other enemies of the party. Soon he was promoted to the imposing post of Assistant Propaganda Chief of the Nazi party. I say that sarcastically because the Nazis were still a long way from power and it's not clear if Himmler had even met Hitler at this time.

"But that was to change soon. Hitler soon gained a strong enough foothold in the government to remove the ban on the Sturmabteilung, the SA, and a fresh recruiting campaign was begun to bring in thousands of new recruits to join these veteran Brownshirts who now reappeared in the streets in masses. I realize many of these details must be confusing you, but I'm sure you've seen Hitler's Brownshirts portrayed in movies?"

"Plenty of times," Sheila said. Matt nodded. Gossick continued.

"The point of all this is that the SS was now seen by Hitler as unnecessary, something that was surely going to fade from view. By this time Himmler and Hitler knew each other casually. Hitler was aware of Himmler's desire for big-sounding titles and promotions. To keep him happy Hitler put him in charge of the SS, giving him the imposing title of deputy leader. Himmler took it as a great honor and a step forward in his career, even though Hitler saw it as a joke. But that 'joke' was to put Himmler in position to carry out the greatest extermination program in human history.

"Himmler seized what was left of the SS and molded them using the highest Nazi racist ideals. It surprised Hitler that this stick figure of a man could accomplish such a feat, and for a while longer he allowed the SS to remain his personal bodyguards, and actually increased their numbers. Perhaps even at this point Hitler knew that he would have to murder his greatest allies, the staff command of the SA in order to seize complete control of the Nazi party.

"This eventually came to pass, and Hitler put Himmler in charge of the slaughter of four thousand leading members of the *Sturmabteilung,* the true legacy of Hitler's years of struggle. It is said that Himmler walked behind his firing squads as they executed the officers, and took notes on which of his men seemed sickened by the bloodshed. Later he was to put those same men up against the walls and have them shot.

"Now there was no stopping Himmler's rise to power, riding as he did on the coattails of Hitler himself. With boring regularity the news announced how Himmler had become Chief of Political Police in a new province. Soon he had taken over the gestapo from Göring, and now even many at the top of the Nazi party trembled. For they began to see Himmler's method—cruelty without conscience. He would do anything for his führer. Indeed, he would commit acts that even Hitler himself was loath to order."

Gossick paused. "Is all this history boring you?"

"No," Sheila said. Matt shook his head.

"But you're wondering what it has to do with what happened to your friend?"

"Sort of," Sheila admitted tactfully.

"I will get to the heart of the matter as fast as I can. But to understand Madame Olga Scheimer, it is necessary to understand who Himmler was, *what* he was. In my mind the two were inseparable.

"World War Two started. Hitler stormed across Europe. It seemed nothing could stop him. All across the continent the Jewish people were rounded up and sent to concentration camps. But Himmler did not describe them that way to the world. He told an assemblage of foreign newspaper men, and I quote, 'The Jews are as much citizens as those of the non-Jewish faith. Their lives and property are equally respected. Protective Custody where it concerns Jews must be understood in this light.' Yes, locking up Jews was called Protective Custody. What irony.

"The oldest concentration camp was founded at Dachau, near Munich, in 1933, before the war began. At first it was used to contain Communists and other political enemies of the Nazi party. Hitler did not begin the extermination of Jews until 1941. It was this year, 1941, that Himmler visited Dachau, and it was here he first met Madame Olga Scheimer.

"The following information I obtained from interviewing SS soldiers who were stationed at Dachau. Many particulars I was able to cross-verify. At the time of her meeting Himmler, Madame Scheimer was the wife of Lieutenant Boris Scheimer, who was in charge of security at Dachau. I was told that Mrs. Scheimer not only lived at Dachau, but helped out from time to time with the executions. Yes, this was a well-educated, well-bred twenty-eight-year-old woman I'm talking about. It was Madame's special pleasure to reassure the naked women who were being herded into gas chambers that they were going for 'wonderful hot showers.' The soldiers I spoke to said Madame was often the first to peek in the chambers when they were reopened after the gas had done its work. Apparently there was something about a mound of tortured corpses that appealed to her sense of delight.

"Himmler met her the first day he arrived at Dachau and shared with her her hideous pastime. I suppose he had finally found a woman he could relate to. Lieutenant Boris Scheimer was immediately transferred to the front lines, where he supposedly died within a month. From that point on, Heinrich Himmler and Madame Scheimer were often together. She traveled with him extensively, particularly when he visited the concentration camps. I was told that it was Madame Scheimer who worked hardest to find the most efficient ways to carry out the Final Solution. I know for a fact she spent months at Auschwitz in Poland, where more than two million died. God only knows what she did there.

"But let me turn to myself at this point. I was a captain under General Patton in what is now called the Battle of the Bulge. I had five hundred men under me and forty tanks. We were the first of the allies to reach Dachau and to liberate the prisoners there. I could spend time going into detail about what we found—the mountains of human ash, the wraithlike survivors. But I think I have already turned your stomachs enough, and to dwell on that time always makes me sick. Suffice it to say no one could imagine the horror that men could do to other men, or that women, one woman in particular, could do to others of her kind.

"Of course that is where I am leading. I do not believe Himmler and Scheimer were human beings as we understand human beings to be."

"What were they?" Sheila asked.

Gossick spoke gravely. "Empty shells."

"Pardon?" Matt said.

"I don't believe there was anything inside them, no soul as we call it. I believe they were simply vehicles for a greater power to work through, an intensely evil power."

"Did you ever meet Himmler and Scheimer?" Sheila asked.

"Yes. I am getting to that. When we arrived at Dachau, in the closing days of the war, Himmler and Scheimer were in Berlin, the last stronghold of Nazi power. There were perhaps a few thousand Jewish prisoners at Dachau who had been kept alive to help bury the dead. I was placed temporarily in charge of taking care of these men and women. It was at the time I met Rabbi Levitz.

"I was drawn to him because he was one of the few survivors who did not have the haunted gaze of the majority. I am not saying he looked well, he was as thin as a skeleton. But he did not look like a beaten man, rather like someone who had gone through a great hardship and emerged stronger. He had a glow, and I don't mean this figuratively. His English was excellent. I liked him immediately and we were soon fast friends.

"Rabbi Levitz was a student of the Cabala—that is the esoteric side of the Jewish faith. I saw him as a modern mystic, and it didn't matter that I had been raised Protestant. We would have long philosophical discussions on the meaning of life, why there was suffering, if there was life after death, reincarnation, and so on. Levitz was Jewish but he was not dogmatic. What I mean is, he used his faith to uncover truth, not to deny other people's truths.

"The reason I called him a mystic is that he could read minds. I mean this literally. I discovered his talent when we played poker. I always lost, and it wasn't because I was a lousy card player. He always knew what I was holding. He finally admitted to me his ability, and then demonstrated a few others, such as the ability to move objects with his mind. But he showed me these things not to impress me, but to open my mind up to possibilities I had not considered before. I asked how he had developed these powers and his answer was simple. By being available, he said. Available to what, I asked. He said he did not know if it had a name. He just allowed his mind to settle, to become still, and made himself available to the power of the universe.

"Naturally I was intrigued, and wanted him to teach me what he could. But he said there was nothing to learn, just knowing that such a thing was possible was enough. He told me to sit quietly, regularly for a period of time and see what happened. I tried this but nothing happened. Maybe it was because I tried too hard—I don't know.

"I have already mentioned how I interviewed captured German soldiers and learned about Himmler and Scheimer's historic meeting. But it was Levitz who provided me with a deeper insight into what these two beings were. Here I must ask your forgiveness ahead of time. What I am going to say next is far from pleasant. I will try to spare you the goriest details and stick to the main points.

"There was a laboratory at Dachau where doctors performed hideous experiments on living people. Levitz had the misfortune of being used in a couple of these experiments. Once one of Himmler's men was trying to determine exactly what electrical voltage was necessary to temporarily short out a person's memory. He was using Levitz as a guinea pig when Scheimer and Himmler walked in.

"They wanted to observe and indicated the doctor should continue. The procedure was extremely painful for Levitz. He joked with me when he told me about it, something about lighting up like a Christmas tree and here he was a Jew. But I think he joked because the horror of it was too fresh in his mind. Yet even with the wires attached to his scalp, and the shots of electricity coming regularly, he was able to observe an interesting phenomena. As he was being tortured, Himmler and Scheimer would close their eyes and smile blissfully as if they were soaking up invisible nourishment."

"What?" Sheila interrupted. "I don't understand."

"I put it poorly," Gossick said. "But Levitz did not know how else to explain it. He said his pain was stimulating Himmler and Scheimer in some primeval fashion, not just emotionally or psychologically. He said his pain was recharging their batteries so to speak."

"They were like psychic vampires?" Matt asked.

"That is an interesting choice of words," Gossick said. "Yes, I suppose Levitz would have agreed with that description. But there is something else. He said that Himmler and Scheimer were empty inside."

"You've said that already," Sheila said. "I'm not sure I understand your point. I can see they were horrible people."

"No," Gossick said firmly. "They were not people. They looked like people, they talked like people, but they were missing something that all people have. They had no souls. They were simply shells that were being used by something else."

"Levitz said this?" Matt asked.

"Yes."

"How could he tell?" Sheila asked.

"He could sense it," Gossick said. "He was a very sensitive man."

"I don't wish to be rude," Matt said, "but it sounds like a purely subjective observation on his part."

"But I told you," Gossick said, "I met them later and felt the same way."

"Tell us about that meeting," Sheila said.

"In a moment. Let me finish with Levitz." Gossick took a sip of his lemonade, puffed on his pipe and then, fortified, continued. "Levitz said that halfway through the shock treatments Himmler suddenly opened his eyes and told the doctor to get another subject. This corresponded, Levitz said, with when he began to pray to God for help. Apparently this prayer broke the flow of energy to Himmler and Scheimer. Indeed, it seemed to make them mad. Scheimer spit on Levitz before she moved onto the next victim. In front of this second poor man, once more, the two stood with their eyes blissfully closed and soaked up the radiations of pain. I'm not sure how Levitz got out of that laboratory alive. This happened two years before we reached the concentration camp.

"I had been at Dachau two weeks when I was

called to Lüneburg, which was under the control of the British. I was told to go to Field Marshal Montgomery's Intelligence headquarters. There Himmler was supposed to be imprisoned. It seemed he had been picked up at a road checkpoint near Bremervorde. At first I didn't know that he had been arrested in the company of Scheimer, but it was no wonder I wasn't told because Scheimer was a nobody as far as British intelligence was concerned. The British were doing the Americans a favor by allowing an American to be present during the interrogation of Himmler. I am not sure why I was chosen, but I suppose I was as qualified as the next man.

"I will never forget the night I was led into the cell where Scheimer and Himmler were being held. I arrived just as they were being stripped naked as part of a personal search. Scheimer was only half clothed when I walked in, and Himmler had only shorts on. Himmler looked as unopposing as a man could: chubby, pale, half blind—this was the monster I had heard so much about at Dachau? I had trouble believing it.

"Scheimer, on the other hand, was a striking woman. Her hair was wonderfully long, light brown, soft like a child's. Her skin was also pale, but seemed to shimmer. I do not mean this crudely, but her body was sensual, and I could see why Himmler, who had had his choice of women, had chosen her. But at first I had trouble reconciling her with the woman Levitz had described in the laboratory.

"Then I looked into her green eyes, and as I did, a faint sneer touched her lush lips. Because she knew I saw her for what she was."

"What did you see?" Sheila asked.

"Nothing," Gossick said.

"How can you see nothing?" Matt asked.

"You don't see it, you sense it. She was like a void. Himmler's eyes were the same, I noticed, when I got a closer look at him. And it was then I set aside any idea that these two were harmless. Staring at them was like looking through a crack in reality. They were alive, they were breathing, talking, but they were not there. All that was inside them was the presence of evil. I tell you, it filled that room like a gaseous cloud. They were simply channels for it."

"Did others feel this presence?" Matt asked.

"Yes. The guards who were watching over the two were pale and shaken when I arrived. And they were the ones with the guns. In fact, I believed if I had not come in when I did, the two might have escaped."

"How?" Sheila asked.

"They were able to manipulate people's thoughts," Gossick said.

"Like Levitz?" Matt asked.

"No," Gossick said strongly. "They were the opposite of Levitz. He had opened himself up to the grace of God and become a greater man for it. He never controlled anyone. These two had opened themselves up to something unspeakable and had lost themselves in it, had ceased to exist as individuals except as instruments of pain."

"Did they manipulate your thoughts?" Sheila asked.

"Scheimer did. I told you she was half naked when I entered, and she sneered at me as I stared into her eyes. Yet as I continued to watch her, I was overcome with the feeling that I had to have her. I mean sexually, and I know what you must think, that I was just another soldier ready to rape an enemy woman. Nothing could be farther from the truth. I had risked life and limb for four years to save people, not to hurt them. But now, here in this prison under Scheimer's wicked stare, I felt I had to get her out of the jail, get her alone and let her show me everything she knew. I went so far as to reach for my pistol, with the intention of pointing it at the guards and demanding that she be turned over to my care.

"But it was then I thought of Levitz. I remembered what he had said when he had told me to sit quietly with my eyes closed and be available to what was there. He had given me one other instruction that had seemed insignificant at the time, which now came back to me with force. He had told me to be available but not to desire for anything for myself, only for the good of all things. That desire came to me right then, and it seemed to break Scheimer's hold on me. Hate filled her face and I grabbed for my pistol, this time to point at her and Himmler.

"It was then Himmler pulled a capsule of cyanide from his shorts and crushed it between his teeth. He had swallowed too much before we could get to him. Cyanide poisoning is not an easy way to die, and it took him several convulsing minutes before he stopped thrashing on the floor. It is interesting to note that Scheimer stood perfectly still all that time, with her eyes peacefully closed. It was as if his pain were a tonic for her."

"What happened next?" Sheila asked. It was a gruesome tale, worse than she had ever heard, but also intriguing. She remembered from her history books that Himmler had killed himself while in prison. But she had never heard any mention of Scheimer.

"Next?" Gossick appeared confused by the question. "There was nothing for me to do next. Himmler was dead. There was no one to question. We removed his body from the cell, locked the door on Scheimer, and I went upstairs to bed. I figured I'd talk to Scheimer in the morning when I felt more myself." He stopped. "But in the morning she was gone."

"She broke out during the night?" Sheila asked.

"No, she was let out," Gossick said. "The British felt they had no authority to keep her locked up."

"But she was Himmler's girlfriend," Matt protested. "She had helped kill people at a concentration camp."

"Yes," Gossick said. "All that is true. But I had not made those facts clear to the British before I went to bed. In my wildest dreams I never imagined they would let her go during the night. Also, I was badly shaken by my encounter with those two. I practically fled from the cell when I got the chance."

"Huh," Matt muttered.

Gossick nodded. "I know it sounds weak. I was weak. Perhaps—and I have wondered about this for many years—I was still suffering from the influence Scheimer had over my mind. Maybe she had consciously blocked me from explaining to the British everything I knew. In either case, she was gone. But I did speak to the British about bringing her back in for questioning. They told me they didn't know where she had gone, that she had left the intelligence quarters with her child and that was that."

"She had a child?" Sheila gasped.

"Yes," Gossick said.

"How old was it?" Matt asked.

Gossick sighed. "A shrewd question, Matt. Was it old enough to belong to Lieutenant Boris Scheimer? Or was it young enough to be Himmler's? When I heard about the child I asked the British officer the same question. His answer chilled me to the bone. The child was only two, a baby girl. Most likely Himmler's own daughter." Gossick shook his head. "Apparently, Scheimer had had the child with her when she was arrested and used her to help persuade the British to let her go, that she was just an innocent mother of an infant. Of course, she had probably used her powerful eyes as well. The British officer I spoke to was responsible for her release, and he was dazed when I spoke to him, as if he could hardly remember who she was."

"Do you know what happened to Scheimer and the child?" Sheila asked.

"I know what happened to Scheimer," Gossick said. "She moved to Los Angeles."

"She moved to Los Angeles after the war and started killing?" Sheila asked.

"Yes," Gossick said.

"Why L.A.?" Matt asked.

"I think it was because she knew I lived there," Gossick said.

10

Dusty Shame lay unconscious on his bed, his ears stuffed with foam rubber plugs, his eyes covered with black daytime sleeper eyeshades. He was asleep but he was not resting. He was having a horrible nightmare.

He was in the cave in the desert at night, buried up to his head in the sand beside all the other corpses. He couldn't budge an inch, which wouldn't have been so bad if a cockroach the size of a German shepherd hadn't wandered into the cave and strolled over to his face. It had the stalest breath, as if it had been eating dead things since the day it hatched. Even that would not have been enough to send Dusty screaming toward waking if the giant bug hadn't started to talk to him in the voice. It was hearing the voice coming out of the mouth of such a filthy thing that made him feel as if his unconscious mind was about to crack open and let out all the demons that had been stored up inside him the whole of his miserable life.

"There are only three fresh bodies here," the cockroach told him in a distinctly feminine voice. He had not realized this about the voice before. "There should be six."

"There are another two down in Pasadena that I wasn't able to get into the trunk of my car," Dusty explained.

"Why not?" the cockroach asked. It leaned forward to get a better look at him and scratched his cheek with one of its antennae in the process. They were very sharp, those antennae. Dusty felt a drop of blood run down the side of his face. He didn't want to make the bug angry.

"One of the girls screamed before I could kill her," Dusty said. "I had to get away from the house. I was afraid the cops would catch me."

"You were afraid, eh?" the cockroach asked, interested.

"Yes, sir."

"Don't call me sir."

"Yes, madame."

"That's better. What were you afraid of?"

"If I got caught by the police they would put me in jail before I could finish killing the six innocents. Then I would never be able . . ." He was afraid to finish.

"Then you would never be able to do what?" The cockroach poked his neck with one of its spiny legs, and Dusty felt a stain of mucus on his throat that burned like acid drained from an old battery as it crawled over his flesh. "Answer me," the cockroach insisted.

"Then I would never be able to silence the voice," Dusty admitted.

The cockroach laughed, the sound not unlike a human giggling—if the human had had a mouth stuffed with sand.

"Do you think you can ever silence it?" it asked.

"I was hoping to," Dusty said.

"Do you know where the voice comes from, Dusty?"

He found it unnerving to be addressed by his first name by the loathsome thing. "No," he said. "Does it come from you?"

The cockroach smiled, which was worse than its laugh. What made it truly sickening was that the smile reminded him of someone he knew. No, he thought, someone he had known long ago. That was an interesting thought, that the voice could have had a human origin. A part of him had always assumed the devil was behind it all.

"Yes," the cockroach said. "But who am I?"

"I don't know."

The cockroach scratched him again, worse this time, across the forehead, so that the blood dripped into his eyes, blurring his vision.

"Answer me!" it demanded.

"I don't know!" he cried. "Stop hurting me!"

"All right, I will stop," the cockroach said calmly, taking a step back. "But only for a few hours. Then I will return for you. And if there isn't another fresh body here by then I will chew off your right ear." It spoke confidently. "You wouldn't like that, not having an ear to hear the voice with, would you, Dusty?"

He didn't completely understand the question because if it only ate one of his ears, he would still have the other. He told it as much, and he probably shouldn't. The cockroach cackled.

"Did I forget to tell you?" it asked. "Before I leave you now I think I'll have a big bite of your left ear."

The cockroach stepped closer and opened its mouth.

Dusty screamed.

He woke up and ripped off his eyeshades and found his mother lying in bed beside him. She had been biting his ear. There was, in fact, blood on his pillow, his blood. The sight of it sent him into a frenzy. He grabbed his pillow and pressed it down over her face. Her limbs thrashed beneath him, her arms even, scratching him, but he held on hard, even with his damaged right hand.

He held the pillow down until his mother's kicking slowed.

Then he realized what he was doing. He loved his mom.

He pulled the pillow away and threw it on the floor.

He popped out his earplugs.

His mother's eyes were open and she was still breathing, but it was coming in painful gasps. His eyes filled with tears and he hugged her.

"Oh, Mom," he cried. "I'm so sorry. I thought you were the cockroach. Come on, don't die on me. Keep breathing, that's it. Your son loves you. He loves you more than anything."

She continued to suck in her pitiful breath, her vacant eyes fixed on his face. Her color was tinged blue as opposed to her usual gray. He worried he might have accidentally crushed her trachea. But she was not turning any deeper blue and that reassured him. He considered for a moment calling an ambulance, but if he had hurt her internally they would get suspicious, and he might end up in jail. That would not do. He had to get that next fresh body immediately, before he even considered going back to sleep again. An ambulance was simply out of the question, he decided. But if he had known mouth-to-mouth resuscitation, he would have performed it on his dear mother. He would have done anything for her.

Dusty got off the bed and went into his bathroom and checked his ear. It was bleeding freely, but most of the ear still appeared to be attached to his head. First Wendy bites him, then his own mom. He grabbed a handkerchief and pressed it over the wound. He could bleed in the car, he had to get out of the house.

It was dark and he had work to do.

Mrs. Garcia glanced up from the living room couch as he went out the front door. He told her that his mom was resting in his bed and not to worry about her, that she was comfortable. Mrs. Garcia gave him a peculiar look, but he did not stop to consider killing her next. He needed someone young, someone whom the voice could not complain about.

He went outside and started his car.

He drove toward Lt. Black's house.

Dixie Black.

11

"I had been working for the L.A.P.D. for over a year when the first girl vanished," Gossick continued. "The circumstances were identical to what happened to your friend. A young woman resting alone in a house, then gone the next day, no signs of struggle, no blood. Just a single card with a swastika drawn on it. I was put in charge of the case.

"It wasn't until the third abduction that I began to think of Madame Scheimer as a suspect. At the time my partners and I had no leads. We were not receiving any ransom notes, we had no fingerprints, we had not even a vague suspect description."

"What made you think of Scheimer?" Sheila asked.

"I guess the obvious answer would be the swastika card, but it's not satisfactory. A truer answer, I feel, would be even more unsatisfactory." Gossick gestured toward the sky with his hand. "It just came to me."

"But why?" Sheila asked again.

"There is no *why,"* Gossick said. "I just felt it might be her. But I can give you a couple of points that led up to this feeling. When the first young woman was taken, I naturally went to the house to search for clues. While I was there, alone in the bedroom, I suddenly felt as if I had been there before. But, of course, I had never been to this girl's house. You see, it was not the house that was familiar to me. It was the feeling in it, the feeling of utter emptiness."

"I felt that way when I entered Nancy's house after she was taken," Sheila whispered. She turned to Matt. "Did you?"

"No," Matt said.

"It occurs when you come up against beings such as these," Gossick went on. "Their touch pollutes. But let me go on. Since I had returned from the war, I had been following Levitz's prescription of getting up early in the morning and sitting quietly with my eyes closed, making myself available to the universal power, desiring nothing except for good things everywhere. I hesitate to say I was meditating for I didn't know what I was doing. I only know that over time I began to experience great peace as I sat there, a joy that would stay with me into the day. And sometimes information would come to me."

"Information?" Matt asked, his tone skeptical.

Gossick nodded. "Information. For example, with these puzzling disappearances I began to receive the impression that Madame Scheimer was behind them all. I can see I'm losing you here, Matt, and I'm not sure if I'm still credible in Sheila's eyes. But this is the simple truth and there is no sense in my trying to dress it up as something else. This is what I tried to tell the two cops who came, and why they laughed at me. You see, I believe that in my battle against this dark force, I was aided by forces of light."

There was a moment of silence. Far away Sheila could hear the faint roar of the ocean waves. Down the street a dog barked, yet the night remained calm, perhaps touched by a particle of the peace Gossick said he had found inside himself. Sheila believed the peace radiated from the old man himself.

"I'm not going to laugh at you," Sheila said. "I grew up watching *Star Wars* movies. This is something Yoda might have said: there is the good side of the Force and there is the dark side."

"Exactly," Gossick said, relieved. "I loved those movies. I owned them and watched them over and over until my VCR ate them. Maybe some time we could all get together and watch them again. But for now I must tell you what I did with my intuitive insights. I decided to try to trace Madame Scheimer's steps from Germany to Los Angeles. I know, I was proceeding on the assumption that she had come to L.A., in Matt's mind surely a huge leap of faith. But I had nothing to lose, we were getting nowhere at the department and by then a fourth girl had been taken.

"I contacted a British Intelligence officer who was still stationed in Berlin, told him all I knew about Scheimer, and asked if he could give me a clue as to how she could have escaped to the U.S. He was intrigued by the fact that she had been Himmler's woman and promised to help. He got back to me a month later—and another abduction later—with the name of a woman who strongly matched Scheimer's description. The woman went by the name of Fraulein Bauer and had boarded a freighter in Sweden bound for Los Angeles. The ship was named the *Triton,* and it had apparently been used to take many refugees of the battle-scarred continent to America. My friend also supplied me with something else—a list of the names of all the people who had sailed with Bauer.

"I tried to contact all the people on the list, but I didn't have my department's help in the matter. They thought I was on a wild-goose chase, and when I tried to explain my reasoning, I lost them altogether. That was a mistake, I realize now, but I couldn't understand how come they couldn't *feel* the truth of my idea. I knew if Levitz had been by my side, he would have felt it. But I was more innocent in those days.

"I had to do all the legwork alone. I didn't have to talk to many people to learn that Scheimer definitely was Bauer. That woman had made an unmistakable impression on many of the passengers aboard the *Triton.* The comments were uncannily similar—she was a cold woman, she was a cruel woman, she was the strangest person I ever met.

"So now I had confirmation that Scheimer had come to Los Angeles. I just needed her address and to follow her around for a few days and then arrest her when she went to kill again. Sounded simple enough. Except Scheimer was not the sort to have confided in her fellow shipmates on her long trip to America. I could find no one, at first, who could tell me where Scheimer settled.

"Then I stumbled across Alex. He was one of the people on my list. I located him through immigration. I can't remember his last name. He was not German but Swedish and should have been repelled by a staunch Nazi like Scheimer. But it seemed he developed an obsession with her while on the boat. In talking to him, I came to believe Scheimer had used her power on him and forced him to become her lover. Perhaps she needed a man to look after her on the long voyage, I don't know. In either case Alex was with Scheimer when she arrived in America. In fact, he lived with her for a month until the night he caught her in bed with another man. It was then Scheimer let him go, and I think I use the correct phrase because I don't think he could have gone anywhere if she had not allowed it. She gave him his freedom on one condition: that he talk to no one about her. If he did, she promised he would meet a bad end."

"Why did he talk to you?" Sheila asked.

"Because he was a frightened man, a ruined man. He had been away from Scheimer several months by the time I got to him, and he said he had not slept a night without terrible nightmares of bugs crawling over him, talking to him, chewing on his body. He was about to blow his brains out when I came to his door. I explained how I believed Scheimer was behind the abductions, and he nodded vigorously. He said she had talked about how nice it would be to kill some innocents again. He knew his problems stemmed from his previous contact with her. He was more than happy to give me her address."

"She was still living in the same place?" Matt asked, amazed.

"Yes," Gossick said.

"But that makes no sense that she would have left someone alive that could so easily point the way to her," Matt protested. "Not if she was as powerful and cunning as you have described."

"It makes plenty of sense if you think that Scheimer had no reason to believe I was on her tail," Gossick said.

"But you said you believed Scheimer came to Los Angeles because she knew you were here?" Sheila asked.

Gossick was thoughtful. "I did say that, didn't I?

I do believe that, too. But I don't know if it was a entirely conscious decision on her part. I honestly don't know if she had a conscious mind as we do. But I feel she came to a place where she sensed she would meet an adversary, someone who would realize who was behind the murders, someone who knew *what* she was. I think for her that was part of the game. But let me answer your original question another way, Matt. I don't think Scheimer believed she had to kill Alex or change her address because she trusted in the evil hold she had over him. And it's true what I said, another few days and Alex would have committed suicide and that would have been the end of any lead to Scheimer."

"What did you do next?" Sheila asked, sitting on the edge of her seat.

"I went to her house and knocked on the front door," Gossick said.

"Wow," Matt said. "That's gutsy. Was she home?"

"She answered the door. She smiled when she saw who it was, or maybe she sneered. Her expressions were difficult to tell apart. She was dressed beautifully, although her home was by no means extravagant. Her long, light brown hair was particularly lovely, I remember, her green eyes. She invited me in and offered me tea."

"God," Sheila whispered.

"I took her up on her invitation. I didn't discuss the murders with her, even though she clearly knew that was why I was there. She didn't mention them to me. Because we both knew I had nothing on her. I couldn't arrest her. Oh, I could have dragged her down to the station and set about trying to prove that she was Himmler's girlfriend and a threat to society. But that would have been difficult without involving numerous European agencies, and Europe was still in tatters at the time. No, I drank her tea and talked with her about the weather, and then I was on my way."

"Was the tea poisoned?" Sheila asked.

Gossick smiled. "No, it was very good if I remember right. But I did not feel well emotionally when I left. I felt psychically drained. She had tried to use her power on me, and it had affected me on a deep level, although I don't think nearly as much as she hoped. You see, I was not afraid to speak to her directly, even after what had happened the night Himmler killed himself. Because I now felt protected. My morning silence periods had given me that assurance."

"But what if she had removed a knife from the drawer while you were in the house and had stabbed you in the back?" Matt asked. "Would you have been protected from that?"

Gossick had to smile again. "It's funny you should ask that question. You'll see why in a minute. But I understand your doubt. No, I think if she had stabbed me, I would have died. But I was not trusting solely in the Almighty. I kept my eye on her the whole time I was with her and made sure she drank tea from the same pot. But let me continue.

"Five girls had been taken already, and I could not directly raise a hand against Scheimer. I had to wait until she tried to kill again. I began to shadow her, and I know what you must think. She must have known I was following her. Of course she knew, it gave her pleasure to have me on her tail. We played a game of cat and mouse for three weeks.

"Then suddenly she left the house in the middle of the night. I followed her at a distance while she entered what is today Orange County, specifically the Irvine area. Back then the place was an endless field of fruit trees, with houses spaced few and far between. She stopped at a small house buried in a field of orange and olive trees. I watched through binoculars as she stepped up to the front door and went inside. That threw me off—the house was unlocked. I figured at first that she was visiting someone she knew. But I didn't figure well. Back in those days people rarely locked their doors, especially out in the country as we were. I sat watching, waiting, and then the conviction slowly swept over me that I was being taken for the greatest fool. Scheimer was committing a crime right beneath my nose. It was what she had wanted to do since she had come to L.A.—to fence with someone on the other side."

"The other side?" Matt asked.

"The good guys," Sheila said. "Let him finish."

"I started my car and raced toward the house. Scheimer was exiting the front door, the body of a young woman in her arms. I had my gun free and ordered her to put her hands up.

"Scheimer was amused. She made me aware of the fact that she had a knife to the young woman's throat and that if I didn't get back in my car and drive away, she would slit the girl's throat. The standoff didn't last long. I had botched it and had no choice but to do what she wished."

"Couldn't you tell the girl was already dead?" Matt asked.

"No. I wasn't sure. I'm not sure to this day that she was. But she probably was."

"Didn't you follow her?" Sheila asked.

"I tried. I lasted only a mile. She suddenly yanked her car off the dirt road into a wooded area, and I lost her in the maze of trees. I didn't find my way out until morning. I felt like such an idiot."

"But you could arrest her now," Sheila said. "You were a cop. You had seen her abduct a young woman."

Gossick was silent a moment, staring at the clouds of smoke that formed around him as he puffed on his pipe. He looked his eighty plus years right then, old and tired. Finally he spoke.

"I could have arrested her, but it would have done no good. She would have found her way out of jail. Certainly she would have had no trouble convincing a jury of her innocence, with her beauty, her style, especially her magnetic eyes. No, I thought the L.A.P.D. would have no more success containing her than British Intelligence. She was Himmler's woman, she was driven by the same force that had allowed him to exterminate six million people in front of the whole world. I considered the matter the whole of the next day. And that night I went to her place and knocked on her door once more. She answered holding her daughter's hand with a smile on her lips. She invited me in for another cup of tea.

"I had never seen her daughter before. She was a beautiful child, close to three now. Her hair was like her mother's, brown silk spun of youth. Scheimer kept her in her arms while she put on the tea and sat at the table beside me. With a straight face, she asked what brought me to the neighborhood.

"I wanted to shoot her right then. I wanted to pull out my gun and put a bullet in her forehead. It was what I had come to do. She was evil, I kept telling myself, she had worked in concentration camps, watched thousands die with glee. She deserved nothing but death.

"Yet I hesitated and I don't know if it was because she was using her power on me or not. It may have been simple human decency that held me back. I looked into her beautiful face and had the hardest time reconciling all I knew of her past with what I was seeing now—a mother with her child. She asked me if I wanted cream and sugar with my tea, and I said both. She brought out a plate of cookies that she had baked that afternoon. When we were almost done with them, and had finished talking about the weather and everything except the previous night, I finally found the strength to blurt out the question.

"'Why?' I said to her.

"'Why?' she repeated back to me. 'Why what, Gary?'

"'Why do you do these terrible things?'

"She did not laugh, as I expected her to. She merely lowered her gaze and rubbed the top of her daughter's head and whispered in the girl's ear. There was something about the way she touched her daughter right then that seemed to break the spell I was operating under. As Scheimer's fingers went through the girl's hair, I couldn't be free of the impression that they were actually razor-sharp talons shearing away the scalp of a screaming infant. The image shook me to the core, it was so strong. Also, her whisper was disturbing. It didn't sound like she used words a human would speak. But then Scheimer raised her head and looked at me once more and said in a soft serious voice, a voice that resonated with a peculiar echo.

"'It goes on in the world. I cannot stop it, I don't want to stop it. You cannot stop it, either. You can bury it and it will take life again. It is a part of life.'

"'It has nothing to do with life, what you do,' I said.

"'That is the question, isn't it? Why it exists? Why I am here, and you are here, and why one of us has to die tonight.'

"And that was her mistake. She told me she was going to attack. I believe she wanted to kill after first making it apparent it was about to happen. I think it heightened the painful radiations for her, and fed her in that black place where she existed. In either case, she suddenly whipped a knife up from beneath the table and moved to stab me in the chest.

"But I had been warned, as I said, and was pushing my chair back as she moved. Her initial swing missed me, but caused me to topple back in my chair. Even as I fell, I reached for the gun in my coat. I heard her call out the strangest thing right then. She said my name. That may not seem strange, but it was the way she pronounced it that struck me. She called to me as if I were her friend. Perhaps she was trying to use the power in her voice to disarm me, I don't know. Clearly I had surprised her by not taking the first stab in the chest.

"But she was not remotely friendly. Even as I somersaulted onto the floor, she tried to stab me again. She had got up so quickly, she had simply flung off her child. The little girl lay sprawled on the floor, weeping. I didn't have time to worry about her. I did a quick flip-flop and kicked my fallen chair at Scheimer's legs. That broke her stride, and she took a second to regain her balance. I used that second to raise my pistol.

"Then time seemed to freeze for a moment. For she saw I had the draw on her, and that all I had to do was pull the trigger and she would join her beloved Reichsführer. There was not a trace of fear on her face. I cannot emphasize this too strongly. Because I have slipped into the error of describing her as enjoying the battle, of being like a normal psychopath, if I can speak that way. But there was nothing in her to fear or to enjoy. As I stared into her eyes in that last second, I saw what I had seen in the prison in Germany. She was a nonentity—a lens for a ray of blackness to focus onto our planet—nothing more. She was not afraid to die because she was not alive.

"I shot her in the chest twice, directly through the heart. She dropped as a normal mortal would, crumpled in a bloody ball on the floor. Her daughter staggered over to her and buried her teary face in her mother's dead face. I remember how the blood soaked up from the floor onto the girl's hair, how the threads caught the sticky fluid and seemed to draw it right up into the girl's brain. And how hard it was to wash out later, that cursed blood, as if it were trying to leave a permanent stain on the girl's life. I picked up the child and carried her out of the house. The shooting had shaken me, but I also felt a profound sense of relief. The monster was dead. I could go back to my life."

"What did you do then?" Sheila asked.

"I buried Scheimer's body in the foothills of the mountains, just outside L.A.. I told my partners what had happened, I felt I had to. There was an investigation, I was supposed to go to jail. But there were men and woman on the force who liked me, people who knew me from the war. Strings were pulled. I was dismissed from the force, but I was not sent to jail." He shrugged. "I was grateful for that. I had done what I knew was the right thing. I couldn't complain about the consequences of my act."

"And the murders stopped?" Matt asked.

"They stopped," Gossick said.

"Until now," Sheila said.

Gossick rubbed his head, showing signs of fatigue. "She said as much. That you could bury it and it would take life again."

"That was just nonsense," Matt said.

Sheila shook her head. "Don't you see Matt that there must be a connection between this story and what's happening now?"

"Where is the connection?" Matt asked. "Scheimer died fifty years ago. She died like the rest of us would have died if we were shot. She has not crawled out of her grave." Matt appealed to Gossick. "You're not suggesting that, are you?"

Gossick reached for his lemonade. "No."

"What became of the child?" Sheila asked.

"Interesting question," Gossick said, taking a sip

of his drink. "Surprisingly, she lived with me for a couple of months until the investigation into my unauthorized activities was complete and the department fully understood that I had killed the girl's mother. That's bureaucracy for you. The adoption people were at the door the next day and the girl was taken from me." Gossick rubbed at his eyes. "It was hard to let her go. We had grown quite fond of her. I called her Tania."

"Tania," Sheila said. "Is that what her mother called her?"

"No. Scheimer had named her Sonia, but the girl didn't seem to mind being called by the new name. We told the adoption agency that her name was Tania. I didn't want any of Scheimer's influence on her."

Sheila stared at Gossick. "Do you believe there was any influence?"

Gossick was evasive. "I don't know what you mean. She was only a child."

"But she was Himmler's and Scheimer's child," she protested. "In your own words two of the worst creatures of this century. How could she have been a normal child?"

"What are you suggesting?" Matt asked.

"Who adopted her?" Sheila asked, ignoring Matt for a moment.

"I don't know," Gossick said.

"You wouldn't have just let her go," Sheila insisted. "I heard it in the way you talked about how Scheimer whispered in her ear, how the blood stained the child's hair. You were concerned about what that child might do when she grew up. What happened to Tania Himmler?"

Gossick cringed. "Don't call her by that name, please. All right, I do know something of what became of her, but not in detail. She was brought up by a family who lived on the coast near Sunset Boulevard. Their name was Jones. Mr. Jones worked as an engineer for a defense contractor. Mrs. Jones stayed home and took care of Tania. The girl grew up to be a perfectly normal person."

"Where is she today?" Sheila asked.

Gossick hesitated. "I don't know."

"How did you lose track of her?" Sheila asked. "Did she get married and move away?"

Gossick hesitated again. "Not exactly."

"What exactly did happen?" Sheila pressed.

Gossick was suddenly pained. "Tania's parents died."

"How did they die?" Sheila asked. "Did Tania kill them?"

"No. But they— Mr. Jones came home one day and shot his wife. Then he put the gun in his mouth and blew his brains out."

"This was a couple the adoption agency chose to raise a child?" Matt asked.

"There was nothing wrong with Mr. and Mrs. Jones," Sheila said firmly, her eyes still locked on Gossick. She sensed what part of the problem was in discussing this matter with the old man. He was trying to protect Tania because he had loved her as a child and didn't want to believe the evil had survived inside his darling. Sheila believed Tania was the connection they had been searching for, although she could not imagine that the woman was directly behind the murders. Tania would have to be what now? Fifty? Kind of old to be out late at night wrestling with the Wendy Barts of the world, Sheila thought.

"I don't know why Mr. Jones did what he did," Gossick said.

"Was Tania living with them at the time?" Sheila asked.

"I believe so," Gossick said. "But I don't know where she went after the death of her adoptive parents. If I did I'd tell you. I don't think she can be easily found. She changed her name after her father lost control. But I don't know what she changed it to."

"But you tried to find out?" Sheila asked. "You were observing her from a distance. Admit it."

Gossick raised an eyebrow. "You are a shrewd young woman, Sheila. But shrewdness is not what allowed me to stop Scheimer. I would not count on it solely to find out who murdered your friend." He added, "Yes, I was watching Tania from afar."

"Why do you think Tania changed her name?" Sheila asked.

Gossick shrugged. "The incident with Mr. Jones was reported in the papers. Maybe she adopted a new identity to avoid the shame. That would not have been an unreasonable act."

Sheila felt her own weariness catching up with her. "There is something we're missing here," she complained. "I feel it's right in front of us, so close we can touch it, but too close to see clearly."

Gossick was intrigued. "I'm sure Yoda and Levitz would tell you to trust that feeling and explore it. You might want to sit quietly for a few minutes with your eyes closed and relax. Sometimes the most insightful thoughts are the ones we don't try to force into our heads. It's almost my bedtime, and I still sit before I retire and have my period of silence. I would be happy to sit with you." He glanced at Matt. "Would you like to join us?"

Matt shrugged. "I won't be getting any divine inspiration tonight. If I close my eyes, I'll just fall asleep."

"Then fall asleep and get some rest," Sheila said, tapping him lightly on the arm. "I want to try this technique of opening myself to the universe."

"Remember to have no personal desire as you sit," Gossick said. "If your head is filled with wants, you never know what you might attract. Just be open to the influence that can uplift the whole of creation. Then relax and let go." Gossick put out his pipe and set it down and nodded to both of them. "Close your eyes."

Sheila shut her eyes and almost immediately felt herself settle down. It was almost uncanny, and she wondered if Gossick's experience with being still was helping her along the path. But maybe it was simply her fatigue taking over, she couldn't be sure.

All her questions slipped away, even as she tried to hold on to them, and she found her breathing slowing down. Time passed, a few minutes, maybe a lot of minutes—it was hard to tell. Her body receded from her awareness and become a distant part of her, not necessarily a large part of what she was all about. She had the faint idea that she was doing this to help people, but the thought itself didn't stay long.

Then she didn't know what she was doing.

She felt as if she were dreaming, but it would be a waking dream because she wasn't asleep. She was out in a desert, and she could see for a thousand miles in every direction. The landscape was enchanting, sculpted only of rock and sand, yellows and reds, valleys and peaks. The sky was clear, the air fresh, a fragrance of daisies in it. The sun was soft on her bare arms and face. Best of all Matt was with her, holding her hand, telling her how much he loved her.

She started to tell him how much she loved him.

Then everything went black, just for an instant.

As if the sun had blinked.

Then the sun returned.

But Matt was gone.

The wind was rising.

It was the wind that brought the storm. The clouds weren't in the sky, they were swept off the ground on the waves of suddenly turbulent air. A hurricane of dust swept over her, beating her, pushing her down, blinding her. The latter was the worst, the dust covering her eyes, because even though Matt had vanished, she thought she could find him again, if she could just see. But the dust storm was like a hand trying to bury everything living in its path. She felt sand collect in her ears, in her mouth, and soon she was choking and falling to the ground. The horror of it all was her utter confusion. Because everything had been wonderful a few moments before. Now she was in hell. But as she fell she let out a cry to God to help her, to please save her and Matt.

Then the dream ended.

And once more she didn't know what she was doing.

She only knew she was floating in a place of peace, a place she never wanted to leave. She may even have *been* the place and the peace, she felt no separateness from it.

But slowly she became aware of her body again. Then she heard Gossick telling her from far away to open her eyes.

She did as she was told and looked around.

Matt was sitting upright and snoring. She left him alone. Gossick was reclining in his chair, an old man ready for bed, but also a kind man who had done a great deal in his life to save people from harm. The warmth that radiated from him was as palpable as the coldness was in Nancy's house the afternoon after she had been taken.

"Well?" Gossick said. "Don't think. Just speak."

"I had a dream."

"What was it about?"

"A storm."

"What was special about this storm?"

"It came out of nowhere—so sudden."

"Like these murders."

"Yes," she said dreamily. "Just like them."

"Go on."

"Nancy personally knew the killer," she said.

"Why?"

"Because she was the only one who didn't have *Einstein.* She was the only one the killer knew personally." The words were out of her mouth before she realized it. "It's so obvious," she gasped at her own revelation.

"It sounds logical," Gossick said, leaning toward her. "What else occurs to you?"

"That Scheimer's influence could have skipped a generation but still have been passed down through her offspring."

Gossick nodded. "I have thought of that."

"How come you didn't mention it?"

"Because I wanted to see if you would think of it." He paused. "You know the other reason, Sheila."

"Are you reading my mind now?"

"No. But you know there is a part of me anxious to protect Tania."

"I understand that. You spoke of her being with you only in passing. But it must have been painful for you to let her go?"

"Yes. I became attached to her quickly." He

glanced at Matt. "You are very attached to this young man."

"Yes."

"And it causes you a lot of pain?"

"Yes." Matt continued to sleep.

"Why?"

"Because I have already lost him." Her voice trembled, the peace she felt left her quickly. "He's leaving me, you see."

Gossick's eyes were kind. "You can take it, Sheila. Everybody will leave you at some time or another. In the end we're all alone. All we have is what we've become during our lives." He paused. "Does that sound cold?"

"No. It sounds true." Sheila closed her eyes briefly. She could not think of her own wishes now, she had to care for her dead friend and the others that might follow her to an early grave. "What would it take for the force you described that worked through Scheimer and Himmler to reappear in the world?"

"Another empty shell," Gossick said.

"How empty?" she asked. It was coming, she could feel it coming.

"Completely empty," Gossick said. "What else was special about your storm?"

"It didn't come from above, it came from below." She paused. "It was a dust storm."

"What does that mean?"

Her body spoke, she did not. It knew more than she, and besides she was about to go into shock.

"It means I know such an empty person," she said.

"Who?"

"You don't know me very well, Sheila. I'm not like the other guys at school."

"Mrs. Shame," she whispered. The empty woman had pointed at her.

"Who is that?"

Mrs. Garcia had been relieved to see her again, still alive.

"My friend's mother. She's only fifty but suffers from Alzheimer's. She's an empty flower." Sheila chuckled bitterly. "Alzheimer's—the name even sounds similar."

"You think she is Tania? Why would you think that?"

"Because I'm not that nice a guy."

The facts were there for her to list. She just had to get them past her choked throat. "Because her son knew Nancy. Because he has *Einstein.* Because he has beautiful light brown hair. Because he has an injured arm, although I think it's his hand that hurts." She glanced at Matt. Her voice was failing her. Some things were just too painful to admit, like lost love, lost lab partners.

"Nancy and I are never going out."

"What is his name?" Gossick asked.

"Dust Storm," she mumbled.

"Pardon?"

She coughed hard, there could have been sand down her throat. "Dusty Shame. He's a nice guy, not completely cold like Himmler and Scheimer. But there's something wrong with him, something even he has told me cannot easily be fixed."

"I'm confused. Why is this boy's mother Tania?"

"There is no why." She tried to smile, even faintly, but could not. "Mrs. Shame is an empty vessel. I think her emptiness has seeped into her son." She stopped. "I think I made a mistake taking him to Lieutenant Black's house."

"You really think this boy is the killer?"

"He is the killer," Sheila said with certainty. The chill she had experienced when she had entered Nancy's house touched her then, just as it touched her when Dusty had reached for her hand in chemistry class. "And he is going to kill again tonight," she said.

12

Dusty Shame parked directly in front of Lt. Black's home, blocking the driveway. It was close to midnight, but it was Saturday night and nearby Westwood Village was bustling. Ordinarily he would never have considered trying to do a job with so much activity going on two blocks away, but to say this was no ordinary night Dusty felt would have been the understatement of the year. He needed a body. His ear was hurting as much as his hand. He couldn't lose any more of his parts. He knew the cockroach had been serious. He was dead meat if he didn't bring it fresh meat.

The lights in the house were on. She was up, that's all he knew. He didn't have time to case the place. He got out of his car and hurried to the side of the house. From there he was able to peek in a window. Dixie was sitting on the living room sofa, talking on the phone. A TV blared in the background. Good, he thought, there was plenty of noise. He glanced around. A wooden fence e closed the backyard. He tried the gate, found it locked. He had already removed his phony cast in the car, but the injury to his right hand would hinder his climbing abilities. She *did* have the TV up loud, he thought. He considered for a moment and then gave the gate a swift kick.

It burst open.

Dixie continued to talk on the phone.

He stepped into the backyard and closed the gate.

He had his hammer and his switchblade in his coat pocket. He had not brought a towel. At this point it didn't matter how much blood he spilled. He didn't even have his garbage bags with him. He was going to have a great time carrying Dixie's body out to his car, he thought. He tried the sliding glass door that led into the kitchen, found it locked, along with all the downstairs windows. He swore under his breath.

But all was not lost. The roof sloped low toward the backyard. He spotted a window on the second floor that was open. Using the fence to give him a boost, he pulled himself onto the roof and up over it, being careful to step lightly. The upstairs window was wide open, except for a screen, which he had no trouble popping free. A moment later he was standing in Lt. Black's bedroom. Lt. Black, the head of the manhunt to track him down. In Dusty's mind it was poetic justice.

He was worried about how to approach Dixie.

Except for Wendy, all his other victims had been asleep. With his injuries he was not at full strength. Even as he stood in the bedroom, he could feel blood trickling from his ear over his neck. Dixie had impressed him as a spunky girl. She could put up a fight, a fight she might win.

He could hear her downstairs, still on the phone, the TV blasting out another one of those dreary videos that always gave him such headaches. He needed to tilt the odds more in his favor. He stepped toward Lt. Black's nightstand. The guy was a cop, he probably slept with a piece.

Dusty found a snub-nosed Smith & Wesson .45 revolver in the drawer.

He picked up the gun, spun the chamber.

Fully loaded.

Dixie was not going to give him a hard time now.

Yet he didn't want to shoot her, not unless he had to.

Guns made a lot of noise.

Then it occurred to him.

Did he have to show her the gun at all?

Maybe he was going about this all wrong.

Maybe he could get her in his car with just a smile.

And kill her later, far away.

Yes!

He could blow her brains out in the cave.

The cockroach would like that.

Dusty stuffed the gun into his coat pocket, beside his hammer and switchblade, and stepped into Lt.

Black's bathroom and checked himself in the mirror. He was not going to get a late-night date looking the way he did. His hair was a mess, he needed a shave, and his ear had bled all over his shirt and coat. He glanced around the bathroom, thought for a moment. Lt. Black was bigger, true, but not by a lot. He could clean up here, find a fresh shirt in the closet, change, climb back out the window and into the backyard, and then ring the front door bell. He could tell Dixie he just happened to be in the neighborhood. She had seemed interested in him that afternoon. She was an airhead and might go out for coffee with him. If she said no, he'd take out the gun.

Dusty closed the bathroom door and turned on the hot water.

He felt a bit better, having a plan.

Ten minutes later he was at the front door wearing a tan turtleneck, his hair neatly combed, his face cleanly scrubbed. He hoped Dixie had not bought her dad the sweater for his birthday or Christmas. He had done a quick bandage job on his ear. He could feel the blood ready to drip out at any second. His mother had chewed up his earlobe. He thought it curious how the cockroach in his dream had threatened to do exactly the same thing. But he didn't have time to think about it long. He rang the doorbell.

He heard Dixie step to the door. "Who is it?" she called.

"Dusty," he called. "Is your dad home?"

She opened the door. She wore gray slacks, a yellow top, her blond hair loose over her shoulders. "Dusty, what are you doing here?"

He smiled warmly. His hammer and knife were now in the car, along with his bloody shirt and coat, but he had the pistol in his back pocket.

"I was in Westwood seeing a movie and thought I'd drop by. I thought if your dad was up, I could show him how to use the computer he said he was getting."

"He hasn't got the computer yet. Besides, don't you remember, I told you he had to work tonight?"

"I forgot. When I saw all the lights on I thought it wouldn't hurt to stop."

Dixie grinned. "Well, I'm glad you did. I've just been sitting here by myself running up the phone bill. Would you like to come in for a soda?"

"I'd like a cup of coffee. I think I need it to make it back to the other side of town. But why don't we go to this place I know that's not far from here? It serves the best cappuccino."

"Awesome," Dixie said. "Come in while I grab a sweater. Oh, I'm still on the phone! Let me say goodbye, it's my friend Lori. I want to tell her I'm going out for coffee with a senior."

Dusty, for the second time that day, entered Lt. Black's house and took a seat on the white sofa, the one he secretly believed he was capable of staining with his filth. Dixie finally bid her friend goodbye, raced upstairs, used the bathroom from the sound of it, then was back downstairs, bouncing like a cheerleader. She definitely had a glow, he thought, and seemed excited to be going out with him, a senior. He opened the door for her as they stepped into the night air.

"I shouldn't be gone long," she said. "My dad might call. He knows I was going to stay up late."

"I'll get you back at a decent hour," Dusty said.

He worried that she might protest his getting on the freeway, especially with Westwood Village and its many coffee shops so close. But he had set her up well with his talk of his favorite place and she didn't complain. Once he had her on the freeway, he knew, she was as good as dead. Because he wasn't going to stop his car until they reached the desert.

She talked and talked as they drove east on I-10, in the direction of Chino. Soon he knew more about her than he wanted to know. She was in a play at school. U2 was her absolute favorite group. She hated rap—it disgusted her. She loved her dad. She loved her cat. She was a natural blond. She didn't have a boyfriend. . . . Did he have a girlfriend?

To give her credit, she did try to find out more about him as well. But he was short on life stories at the moment. Besides, her voice was beginning to annoy him. Sitting in the car with Sheila had been so much more pleasant. Dixie didn't know that there was such a thing as pausing to catch your breath. His headache began to return about the same time she wondered out loud where they were going. They had just passed downtown L.A.

"It's not much farther," he said.

"What city is it in?" she asked.

"I don't know. It's not far."

"You don't know what city it's in?"

"I just said that, didn't I?" he snapped.

That quieted her for a moment. "It's just like I said, my dad might call while I'm out. If I'm not there, he'll worry."

He may as well start now, Dusty thought.

"We won't be out that late," he said.

She checked her watch. "Boy, it's twelve-thirty already."

"That ain't late."

"Maybe for you, but for me it's practically the middle of the night. Believe it or not, I usually go to bed at nine-thirty. I have rehearsals in the morning before class. I have to get up when the sun rises."

"That's rough," he said.

"If you'd like, you can come to my play. It opens this week. I'd love to have you there." She paused. "Do you think you could make it?"

"No."

"Oh. Why not?"

"I have stuff to do."

"What kind of stuff?"

"I don't know."

"You don't have to go this next week. You could go the week after next. The play runs for a month.

It's called *Lu Ann Hampton Laverty Oberlander.* It's about this woman named Lu Ann. I play her daughter. You'd love it, I know you'd love it. Should I get you a ticket? I can get them free."

Dusty put his sore hand to his pounding head. He had finished off his bottle of Tylenol on the way to Dixie's house and had not taken the time to stop for more. There was something about the girl's voice, a whiny quality, that scraped at his nerves. She had not been such a pain in the ass that afternoon.

"What night would you like to come?" she asked.

"Would you shut up, please," he said suddenly.

That silenced her for a grand total of five seconds. "What's wrong, Dusty?" she asked softly.

"Nothing."

"You seem in a bad mood."

"I'm not in a bad mood."

"Is your arm bothering you?"

"No."

"Hey, wait a second. What happened to your cast?"

"I took it off."

"Your arm is better already?"

"Yes."

"What happened to your ear?"

"I hurt it."

"How come your hand's bandaged?"

"Because I hurt it."

"How did you hurt it?"

"I was wrestling with a girl and she bit me."

"What?"

"Would you just close your goddamm mouth!" he shouted. God, she was like a broken record. Maybe he should just put a bullet in her brain now, he thought, put them both out of their misery. She sank back in her seat at his outburst.

"You *are* in a bad mood," she said, her voice quivering. She sniffed and glanced at the freeway signs. "I think I should go home now. I don't want any coffee."

"No."

"I mean it, Dusty. I should get back. I didn't know you'd take me this far out."

"We are not going back."

She paused, eyeing him. "What do you mean?"

He gave her a stern look. "Exactly what I said. I'm not taking you home tonight. Now you're to sit there quietly and not make another sound. If you do, you will make me mad. And you don't want to make me mad, Dixie, believe me."

She lasted ten seconds this time before speaking. But Dusty was prepared for her. He had already slipped the pistol into his left hand. When she opened her mouth, he swung his arm around and struck her in the face. He caught her between the nose and the mouth, real hard. Her head snapped back and blood from her nose splashed over her blouse. A muted cry escaped her lips. But Dixie didn't shut up that easily. She was stunned, but two seconds later he could see she was preparing to scream. He quickly switched the gun into his injured right hand and pressed the nozzle into her left ear.

"If you make another sound," he said softly, "if you say even one word, I will put the bullets in this gun into the center of your brain. Do you understand me, Madame Dixie?"

Her eyes were the size of Ping-Pong balls, the color of glass. She nodded weakly.

He lowered the gun. "Good. We have a drive ahead of us. We're going to the desert." He nodded ahead at the road. "And in case you're wondering what's out there, but are afraid to ask, I'll tell you." He was suddenly in a good mood. He had his sixth innocent. The voice would be pleased. Soon he would be free. He didn't have a body bag for this one, the insects would get to her right away.

"Cockroaches," he told her.

13

Sheila Hardholt had been only thirty feet away when Dusty Shame had taken the lieutenant's pistol and struck Dixie Black in the face. The savage blow had made her heart skip, and there had been no one at her side to reassure her. She was alone in her own car, trailing the two in the same lane of the freeway, but to where she didn't know.

A string of fortune and misfortune had brought her to her current situation. After realizing who the killer was, Sheila had awakened Matt. He had listened to her theory with a surprisingly open mind. And why not, he had always thought Dusty was weird. Plus Gossick had backed up her reasoning as entirely logical. They had hurried inside to call Lt. Black at all three of his numbers. Right away they had run into problems.

First they dialed the number that was supposed to beep Lt. Black, leaving an urgent message for him to return their call immediately. After ten minutes he still had not called back. Next they tried his home number, but it was busy, and it remained busy. Finally Gossick called the police department directly and tried to hunt down Black. He was told the lieutenant was in the field. Gossick asked for anybody who was working on the murder case with Lt. Black. He was told that all of Black's people were in the field, but that they could take a message for him. Gossick looked stumped. Sheila suggested the police send a car to Lt. Black's and Dusty Shame's houses right away. Gossick relayed the first part of the message. The person on the other end wanted to know Lt. Black's address.

"Don't they know it?" Sheila complained.

Gossick put his hand over the phone. "The L.A.P.D. is huge. The person we're talking to doesn't even know who Lieutenant Black is. She just knows how to switch us to his office. But no one is picking up there. It's late. You said you were at his house today. Don't you know the address?"

"I don't have it memorized," Sheila said. "I had it written down on a scrap of paper." She searched her pockets. "It might be in the car. Have them hold, let me look."

But she couldn't find it, even with Matt's help. They were back inside a few minutes later. Gossick was still on the phone.

"I don't know where it is," Sheila said. "But I think I could get to the place from memory."

"Could you describe how to get to it?" Gossick asked.

"No. I don't know the names of the streets on that side of town."

Gossick spoke to the woman on the line. "We don't know the address of the house, but the lieutenant works for the L.A.P.D. You must have it on file. What do you mean you don't have access to those files? Who does? This is an emergency—we can't wait until tomorrow."

Gossick got nowhere with the woman, even after another ten minutes of trying. Frustrated, he left a message that he was to be called the instant one of Lt. Black's people checked in. Sheila tried to stop him as he set down the phone, but he held up his hand.

"I know I didn't ask them to send a car to Dusty's house," he said. "We'd have to call the San Bernadino police to do that, and I don't know if I want to call them yet."

"Why not?" Matt asked. "Dusty could kill someone tonight."

"I am aware of that possibility," Gossick said. "But we will not be able to convince just anybody over the phone how dangerous Dusty is. If a police car is sent to his house, and he's there, it will just serve to warn him that we're on his tail. You see, the police will not be able to arrest him just because we happen to call and say he is a bad person. They don't know us from Adam."

"But you said you have friends who still work for the L.A.P.D.," Sheila said. "Can't you call them? Won't they believe you?"

"They may believe me, if I can get to them, but then they'd have to convince the San Bernadino police who Dusty is. No, I think if we do all that, we'll end up in the same boat—with a black and white unit stopping by Dusty's house to have a chat with him. After that, Dusty will probably flee the area, only to start killing elsewhere. Sheila, only Lieutenant Black would be able to understand your reasons for why you suspect Dusty. He is the one we want to confront Dusty. He may have annoyed me while he was here, but I could see he was a good cop."

"But he's not calling us back," Matt protested. "He may not call us for hours."

Gossick frowned. "I know. We may have to go to Dusty's house ourselves. I still have my police revolver."

"Is it fifty years old?" Matt asked.

"Yes. But it killed one monster. It can kill another."

"I don't want Dusty killed," Sheila said. "He's sick, he needs help."

"If he's even the one who's behind all this," Matt muttered. He held up his hand as Sheila started to protest. "I agree that he probably is the killer, with all the coincidences you explained. But in my book he's not guilty until proven guilty." He turned to Gossick. "You would agree?"

"I am not going to shoot the young man unless he tries to harm one of us," Gossick said. "I probably would not have harmed Scheimer if she hadn't attacked me."

"You want the three of us to drive to Dusty's house now?" Sheila asked.

"I think that's the best plan," Gossick said. "I'll make sure he stays put until Lieutenant Black can speak to him."

"But I'm worried about Lieutenant Black's daughter, Dixie," Sheila said.

"Why her?" Matt asked.

"Two reasons," Sheila said. "Lieutenant Black made it clear while we were there that he had to work tonight, that Dixie would be alone. Also, when we first entered the house, I asked Dusty what he thought of Dixie and he said, "She looks innocent."

"So?" Matt asked.

Gossick nodded gravely. "Scheimer went after complete innocents. It was part of her pattern. Hitler and Himmler went after the Jews for no reason at all. Sure, they made up ones, but it was because they were innocents."

"It was also the way he said it," Sheila said. "In a weird voice. In retrospect, it was almost as if she fit a category he was filling." She paused. "We have to go in two cars. I'll go to the Blacks' house. You two go to Dusty's."

"No," Matt said firmly. "If we go to the Blacks' house, we'll go together."

"I agree," Gossick said. "If this boy has the same

force working through him that Scheimer did, he is more dangerous than any killer in the last fifty years."

"No," Sheila said. It was there again, the feeling of certainty that Gossick had spoken about having when he was a young man. "You two must go to Dusty's now. It is the more dangerous place. But I know, Gossick, I *know,* I have to go see Dixie and that I must leave now."

Gossick studied her. "You are being led to go there?"

"Yes."

"But you feel there is danger there as well?"

Sheila felt a slow panic growing. "I can't explain how I feel. I only know we must stop talking and leave now. You have a car, Captain?"

He smiled at the title. "I have a fine car. It can take us to Chino. But I'm still hesitant to let you go by yourself. You take Matt with you, and give me directions to Dusty's house."

Sheila began to back away from the two of them, as if pulled by an invisible string, a puppet's string, but hopefully one controlled by a kinder master than the puppet master that tugged on Dusty's strings.

"I'm sorry I can't talk about this anymore," she said.

"Sheila," Matt protested, moving to stop her. But Gossick stopped him.

"Let her go," he said.

Matt shook free. "I don't agree with all this

World-War-Two-Star-Wars-trust-in-the-Force B.S. Sheila, you're acting like a nut. Give me your car keys."

"Bye," she said. She fled out the front door, Matt chasing after her. But he must have tripped on the porch steps or something because she gained extra strides on him and was able to get inside her car and lock the door before he could catch her. He pounded on her window.

"Sheila! Stop!"

She started the car and smiled and blew him a kiss. Then she backed up sharply, throwing him off balance. She was out in the street and speeding away before he could recover.

She found Lt. Black's house easily.

Dusty's car was parked out front.

So it was true.

She had known it had to be.

Yet the confirmation almost shattered her.

Dusty had killed Nancy. He had done them all.

She watched and waited for only a minute, on the verge of going to the nearest phone booth and calling the police, when Dusty strode out the front door with Dixie beside him. Right then Sheila thought of slamming her car into Dusty's, leaping out, and screaming for Dixie to flee. Fear kept her in place. They were next door to Westwood Village. There were hundreds of people out late. Yet there was no one else on the block at that moment. She didn't know how well armed Dusty was. But she knew one thing for sure. He was capable of killing two girls at once. She watched as he opened his car door for Dixie. He climbed in his side, then drove away. She followed, keeping her distance. She followed him right onto the freeway and realized she might have made a terrible mistake not trying to stop him when she had the chance. She wished more than anything that she had a car phone. She had a feeling Dusty was taking Dixie to a place where there would be no public pay phones.

Then miles later, on Highway 10, in the glare from her headlights, she saw Dusty strike Dixie.

Her guilt weighed on her like a second broken heart.

She could only follow, and hope, and pray.

14

Matthew Jaye and Captain Gossick reached Dusty Shame's house about the same time Sheila Hardholt witnessed Dusty's striking Dixie Black. They had driven at an average speed of over a hundred miles an hour to get to Chino, and they had spent half the time marveling about how lucky they were not to have gotten a ticket. Matt, who was behind the wheel, still didn't believe in the Force, but he was beginning to wonder what the hell was going on. He had yet to forgive himself for letting Sheila slip through his fingers so easily. But he did feel Dusty's house would be the more likely place for trouble if there was to be trouble.

Gossick began to load his revolver as they exited the freeway. Matt didn't know how he had hidden the weapon from Madame Scheimer when he had gone to her house for tea and shot her that night almost fifty years ago. The gun looked like a cannon.

"You only have to shoot somebody once with this thing," Gossick agreed when Matt told him what he thought.

"But you said you shot Scheimer twice?"

"I wanted to be sure, son."

They parked three houses down the street from Dusty's and approached the place cautiously. There was no car in the driveway, but there could have been one in the closed garage. Matt hardly knew Dusty. He certainly didn't know what he drove. There appeared to be a light on in the living room, but the drapes were drawn. Gossick suggested they knock on the front door. The man had not changed his style in all these years, Matt thought. He liked Gossick, never mind the old guy's funny ideas on things. Gossick had his revolver hidden, sort of, in his belt under his coat.

"All right," Matt said. "Let's do it."

A short Hispanic woman answered. Matt couldn't tell if she was relieved to see them or terrified. It seemed a combination of both. She was dressed; they had not dragged her out of bed.

"Is Dusty here?" Matt asked.

She shook her head tightly. "No."

"Do you know where he is?" Matt asked.

"No."

"Do you know when he'll be back?" Matt asked.

"No."

"Do you speak English?" Gossick asked.

She held up her thumb and index finger an inch apart. "Little bit."

"What is your name?" Gossick asked.

"Mrs. Garcia."

"Pleased to meet you, Mrs. Garcia," Gossick said, offering his hand, which she shook reluctantly. "My name is Gossick. This is Matt. He goes to school with Dusty. We're sorry to bother you so late, but it's important. Is Dusty's mother here? I would like to see her."

"She is—bed," Mrs. Garcia said.

"Would it be possible to wake her?" Gossick asked. "I know her from a long time ago."

Mrs. Garcia cast a worried glance over her shoulder. "She—in Dusty's bed. I don't know—sick."

"She's sick?" Gossick asked.

Mrs. Garcia shook her head miserably. "Don't know."

Gossick pushed his way through the front door. "We must see her then if she's sick. Shh, don't worry, Mrs. Garcia. We are only here to help."

They found Mrs. Shame dead on Dusty's bed.

She lay on her back, her eyes and mouth open wide.

Matt stood by Dusty's desk, beside Dusty's computer. He had just turned on the light.

Gossick stood at the foot of the bed, staring at the dead woman.

Matt was surprised to see a tear on his face.

"It's Tania," he said sadly.

"You recognize her?" Matt asked. After all these years?

"Tania, yes," Mrs. Garcia said anxiously. "She is sick."

Gossick reached out and closed the dead woman's eyes. He closed her mouth and then kissed her gently on the forehead. "Tania," he whispered.

"Gossick?" Matt said.

Gossick stood. His face was pale. "Sheila was right, I did love her. A long time ago." He turned to Mrs. Garcia. "Mrs. Shame is dead, Mrs. Garcia. Do you understand?"

Mrs. Garcia nodded weakly. "Understand. Dead."

"Do you know how she died?" Gossick asked.

The woman shook her head quickly.

Gossick took a step toward her. "Did Dusty do anything to her?"

Mrs. Garcia's eyes were wide with fear. "He bleeding when he go."

"He was bleeding?" Matt asked.

"Here." Mrs. Garcia touched her right ear.

"Do you have any idea where he went?" Gossick asked.

She shook her head.

"Did he go out at night a lot?" Gossick asked.

"Yes."

"Do you know where he would go?"

"No." Mrs. Garcia paused. "Desert."

"He would go out to the desert?" Gossick asked.

"Yes."

"How do you know?" Gossick asked.

"Follow," Mrs. Garcia said.

"You followed him?" Gossick asked.

"Yes."

"Why did you follow him?" Gossick asked.

Mrs. Garcia touched a hand to her head, as if simply living in the house had been a great trial for her. "I scared," she said.

"You were scared of what he was doing in the desert?" Gossick asked. "You wanted to find out what he was up to?"

Mrs. Garcia nodded. Her face was damp. "Yes."

"Could you take us to this place in the desert?" Gossick asked.

"No."

"Why not?" Gossick asked.

"Don't know—" She gestured helplessly. "Don't know."

"You know he went into the desert, but you don't know exactly where he went in the desert?" Gossick asked. "Is that right?"

"Yes."

"Could you take us close to the place in the desert?" Gossick asked.

She wiped at her face. "Scared."

"You don't have to be scared, Mrs. Garcia," Gossick said. "I am a police officer. I have a gun. I can protect you. It is very important we go to this place in the desert."

"But—don't know."

"I understand. You only know roughly where to go?"

"Yes."

Gossick turned to Matt. "We should call Lieutenant Black's house to see if Sheila is there."

"That's what I've been dying to do since we got here," Matt said. He took out the card Lt. Black had given him. Dusty had a phone in his room. He dialed the number. A man answered.

"Hello?"

"Is this Lieutenant Black?" Matt asked.

"No. Who's this?"

"My name is Matthew Jaye. I'm trying to get hold of Lieutenant Black. It is very urgent."

"Are you one of the people who called and wanted a police car sent to his house?"

"Yes. We're the ones who have been leaving messages for him. Is he there? Is his daughter there? Is Sheila there?"

"Who's Sheila?"

"My girlfriend," Matt said. "Who are you?"

"I'm Officer Wilson. I was dispatched here by Lieutenant Black to check on his house and his daughter. He must have got one of your messages. But his daughter is not here."

"Is Sheila there?"

"There's nobody here."

"Are there any notes lying around?"

"Not that I can see."

"Does Lieutenant Black know his daughter is gone?" Matt asked.

"I was just going to call him. If you would like to speak with him, I can have him call you."

"Yes. It is very important he call us immediately." Matt turned to Mrs. Garcia. "What is the number here?"

She answered without hesitation. "Five five five —six two four two."

"I heard it," Officer Wilson said on the other end. "I'll beep him now and have him call you."

"Thanks." Matt set the phone down and turned to Gossick. "Dixie's not there. Neither is Sheila."

Gossick frowned. "It's possible the two of them went out to a coffee shop to get away from the house."

Matt shook his head, pacing. "She would have left a note. I don't like this, Gossick. What if she got there when Dusty was there?"

"We don't know if Dusty went there."

"Of course he did!" Matt shouted. "Dixie wouldn't have got up in the middle of the night and gone out. Sheila was right. Dusty wanted to dust Dixie."

"Then it's important that we get out to the desert," Gossick said. "If this is where he takes the girls."

Matt felt as if he was going to explode. His girl with that bastard! Now that she might be in danger, he couldn't stop thinking of her as his. He pointed a finger at Mrs. Garcia.

"She's not going to be able to lead us to him," he said. "It sounds like she just followed him for a bit and found out the general direction he went in."

"Highway Fifteen," she said suddenly.

"Dusty would drive out Highway Fifteen late at night?" Gossick asked. Mrs. Garcia nodded solemnly.

"Highway Fifteen," she said. "Then Highway Three Ninety-five."

"It sounds as if she knows where she's going," Gossick said.

Matt moved toward the door. "Good. Let's get out of here."

"Maybe we should first wait for Lieutenant Black to call," Gossick said.

Matt slapped his leg with his fist. He had never felt this wired in his life, or this helpless. He was going to get to Sheila, whatever it took he was going to get her back safe. "I'm not waiting," he said.

The phone rang.

Gossick answered it.

"Black? This is Gossick. Matt and I are at Dusty Shame's house, the boy you met this afternoon. We have strong reason to believe he is the one behind these killings, but I do not have time to explain all our reasons. Yes, I know your daughter has disappeared. We believe it's Dusty who took her. We also think Sheila might be with them. Listen to me, Lieutenant! Don't despair. We think we know where he might have taken the girls. Dusty's live-in housekeeper is here and she has followed Dusty into the desert at night. Go north on Fifteen to Three Ninety-five. Right there, you can only go north on Three Ninety-five. We're going to drive to the desert right now. No, we don't know how far up

Three Ninety-five we have to go, but we have Mrs. Garcia to help guide us. Where are you? No, we can't wait for you. Yes, I know you'll get lost. We might get lost as well, but we can't wait for you to drive here from L.A. I know how fast your cars are. Look, I have a box of flares in the back of my trunk. If I find where Dusty has taken the girls, I'll shoot one off. In the desert at night it will be visible for many miles. No, we cannot wait. We have to go. I have a gun, Lieutenant, I haven't forgotten how to use it. If I find Dusty, I'll stop him. That is a promise I make you. I'm putting down the phone now. Let us pray for the safety of both the girls."

Gossick set down the phone.

"He wanted to come with us?" Matt asked.

"You can imagine," Gossick said. He nodded to Mrs. Garcia. "Let's hit the road."

15

Dixie Black had stopped talking, but she was still more trouble than a dead body. When Dusty Shame reached his favorite parking place in the desert, a half mile shy of the opening of the cave, he stopped and got out and went around to the passenger's side. He motioned with his gun for Dixie to get out as well. But she wouldn't. She was hanging on to her seat as if she were aboard a jet airliner that had just blown out a window at high altitude and was losing everything in the cabin because of the tremendous vacuum suction. Dixie looked as if she'd die if she let go of the seat. Of course, Dusty couldn't blame her for that because it was true. He pressed the gun close to her head.

"You can talk now if you don't scream," he said. "But you still have to do what I say or I'll kill you."

Her face was teary, but her nose had stopped bleeding, and she had wiped away most of the gook. "What are you going to do to me?"

"We're just going for a little walk is all."

"Are you the guy who's killed all those girls?"

A part of him had always wanted to tell somebody. "Yes."

She wept. "Oh God."

"Wherever I am, Dixie, God keeps a distance. There's no use praying to him now." He lightly tapped her head with his gun. "Get out of the car now or your brains will be on the seat in three seconds. One—two—"

Dixie got out of the car. They walked toward the cave. It was late at night but still earlier than the last time he had been in the desert with Nancy's body. The half moon was still in the sky to guide their steps. But Dixie proved to be a real klutz when it came to hiking. She kept tripping over loose stones. Once again he wished he was just carrying her body. It would have been more work, but he believed his mind would have been more at ease. He had lost his smile an hour ago in the car.

They reached the cave.

Dixie did not want to go inside.

But what she wanted was not important.

He led her with his flashlight to the rear of the cave, where the bodies were buried. Dixie walked ahead of him crying. When she reached the final wall, she just stood there sobbing and wouldn't turn around.

"Dixie," he said, standing three feet behind her, his gun hanging by his side.

"Yes?"

"You are the sixth one."

"Oh God."

"You are the sixth girl I have killed. When I kill you, I'll be finished. I won't have to kill any more. I'll graduate from school and probably go to college. I'll get a normal job. Maybe I'll get married and have children, I don't know." He paused. "I just wanted to tell you that."

She turned slowly, her face a mask of shadows and fear in the beam from the flashlight. She was shaking badly. "Are you going to shoot me?" she asked.

"Yeah. In the head. But I can shoot you in another spot if you want." He raised the revolver. "This is your father's gun, by the way."

She cringed, moaning. "No, please, don't hurt me. You can't hurt me."

"If I shoot you in the head, I don't think there'll be any pain."

She dropped to her knees, her trembling hands clasped together. "Please don't kill me. For the love of God."

"I don't know what that is, Dixie. I honestly do not." Dusty cocked the hammer. "Goodbye. I'm sorry we're both going to miss your play."

Dixie pressed her hands to her face and closed her eyes.

Dusty put pressure on the trigger.

Number six, he thought. It's over.

But it was not over.

"Dusty," a voice called from the mouth of the cave.

Sheila Hardholt had almost lost Dusty Shame when he had taken his sudden turn off 395. Because she had been keeping her distance, not wishing to alert him, he had been a couple of ups and downs on the wavy road ahead of her. Then, when she had crested one peak, his car had simply vanished. For a moment she thought she had blown it. Then she noticed his taillights far away, off to the right, plowing through a self-created dust storm. When she reached the spot where he had left the road, she killed her lights and reduced her speed. In the distance she had seen him make another turn, this one to the right as well. Then, a minute or two later, she had seen the red flash of his brake lights. She had parked at that point and followed him on foot, maybe a quarter of a mile behind him and Dixie, their figures like the shadows of two silver ghosts floating lost in the moonlight. She had been relieved to see Dixie still on her feet.

But the time for all relief was past.

She stood at the entrance to the cave and heard Dixie's pleas.

She heard Dusty's flat responses.

She realized the danger.

If she spoke, she would almost certainly die.

They would both die. It was madness to do anything.

Yet.

"You are the sixth girl I have killed. When I kill you, I'll be finished."

She owed it to Lt. Black to do what she could.

His daughter was his life.

She called out Dusty's name.

"It's me, Sheila," she said.

Dixie suddenly stopped crying.

Dusty muttered something under his breath.

Sheila walked into the cave.

The stone roof was low at first, and she had to crouch as she moved. Soon, though, she was able to stand and walk freely. She noticed the abrupt drop in temperature relative to the outside air. She had no doubt she was in the place where Scheimer and Dusty took their victims.

But what about her own fear? Was it so intense that she could hardly walk? Or was she in shock and didn't feel a thing, never mind know what she was doing? She supposed it was a combination of both. Plus a third element. The magic Gossick had spoken of, the feeling of protection—it surrounded her like a protective aura. Yet she did not trust in it altogether because she didn't believe it could repel bullets. From listening to him speak to Dixie, she knew he had a gun. All things considered, she figured she was walking to her death, and she was terrified.

Dusty shone his flashlight on her as she reached the rear of the cave. Half blinded, she raised her arms and gestured for him to turn it aside. He complied with her wish. As her vision cleared, she noticed signs of recent burials. Her fear went up another notch, and it had already passed the top two hours ago.

Dixie knelt on the fine white sand, a lump of misery, Dusty standing before her like a vision from hell. His ear was bleeding, his gun was black, and the emptiness in his eyes reminded her of the stare of a huge insect. At last she understood what Gossick meant when he had described the look in Himmler's and Scheimer's eyes.

"Hello, Dusty," she said.

He took a breath. "What are you doing here, Sheila?"

"You know what I'm doing here. I have to stop you."

"I can't let you do that."

"Why not?"

"I have to kill this girl. I probably have to kill you. Why did you come, Sheila?"

"Because what you are doing is wrong. It doesn't matter how many you kill, it will not be right. You will not be right. You're sick and you need help. Let me help you." She took a step closer. "Give me the gun."

He shook his revolver. She halted.

"You don't understand," he said.

"I do understand. You feel you have to kill six people, six innocents. You feel if you execute Dixie, things will be better for you. But they will only be worse."

He was curious. "How can you be sure of that?"

"Think, Dusty. Each time you've killed, has it gotten any better?"

He considered her question. "No. But that was because I wasn't through yet. If I shoot Dixie, it will have to get better."

"If you shoot Dixie, you will have to shoot me," Sheila said.

He lowered his head. "I don't want to hurt you."

She took another step toward him. "If you shoot me in the head it shouldn't hurt," she said sarcastically.

He whipped his head. "Don't mock me!"

"Don't kill her!" she yelled back. "Let her go."

He was suddenly upset. She welcomed the change, anything was better than that blank stare.

"Don't you see I can't let her go? That I'll go crazy if I don't finish this?"

She spoke evenly, seriously. "Who promised you that if you killed six it would be finished?" she asked.

He hesitated. "The voice."

"What voice?"

"The voice that talks to me." He added, as if embarrassed, "I don't know where it comes from. But it might have something to do with a cockroach."

She frowned. "What cockroach?"

"The one in my dream. I had it this afternoon. It was the first time I dreamed about something that spoke with the voice. It told me I had to kill the sixth girl right away. It said if I didn't, it would come back for me and eat off my ear. That scared me and I woke up." He paused, puzzled. "My mom was in bed with me. She was chewing on my ear." He gestured to the bloody mess at the side of his head. "Can you believe she did that to me?"

"As Scheimer's fingers went through the girl's hair, I couldn't be free of the impression that they were actually razor-sharp talons shearing away the scalp of a screaming infant. The image shook me to the core, it was so strong. Also, her whisper was disturbing. It didn't sound like she used words a human would speak."

The voice. Who was the source of the voice?

"I remember how the blood soaked up from the floor onto the girl's hair, how the threads caught the sticky fluid and seemed to draw it right up into the girl's brain. And how hard it was to wash out later, that cursed blood, as if it were trying to leave a permanent stain on the girl's life."

"I believe it," Sheila said. She moved to within three feet of Dusty, all the time staring him right in the eyes. Yes, the more she focused on him, the more pain appeared, yes, but also the more life lit up inside him. The Force was not strong in her family. She was not Yoda, or even Luke Skywalker. She could not just zap him with her mind. But she could understand him, and maybe that's all he needed right now.

"Stop," he warned her.

She stopped. "I know where the voice comes from."

He blinked. "Where?"

"The past. I met a gentleman tonight who knew your grandparents. He knew your mother as well. But your grandparents—they weren't nice people. Your grandmother in particular was a bad influence on your mother. But the influence didn't emerge until the Alzheimer's disease ruined your mother's brain and allowed the bad thing from the past to come into the present. Tell me, Dusty, did you ever hear the voice when you were away from home?"

He was listening to her. "No."

"When would you hear it?"

"When I was trying to sleep in my bed. It would come, it wouldn't let me sleep." He winced. "You have no idea how awful it was."

"Was the voice in your head?"

"I don't know. It was just there, telling me to kill." He looked at her pleadingly. "I had to do what it told me. It wouldn't stop unless I did."

"I understand. Did you ever open your eyes when the voice was talking to you?"

He shook his head. "I couldn't do that."

"Why not."

"It told me if I did, it would eat my eyes out." His face screwed up in pain. "It would eat my eyes, it would eat my ears."

"Dusty, it was your *mother* who was talking to you."

Dusty did a double take. "What?"

"Your mother was the source of the voice."

He froze for an instant. "But my mother cannot speak. She has not spoken in years."

"Something speaks through your mother. The voice of your mother's mother. A woman named Madame Scheimer. Scheimer was your grandmother. She was an incredibly evil woman. She uses your mother."

"How do you know her?" Dusty asked.

"I told you, I met a man tonight who knew her. His name is Gossick. He worked for the Los Angeles Police Department and shot and killed Scheimer fifty years ago because she had murdered six young women. Don't you see, Dusty, Scheimer is forcing you against your will to do what she did. But you don't have to do it."

Dusty was thinking, it was good to see him thinking. "Did this Gossick bury Scheimer's body?"

"Yes."

"Where?"

"In the San Fernando foothills," Sheila said.

She had hit the bull's-eye. Dusty almost fainted. He staggered back, actually bumping Dixie, who was sitting so still she might have already been dead. But the girl gave a start as Dusty touched her. Sheila motioned for her to remain still. Dusty collected himself once more, but he had lowered his gun.

"What you say is true," he said.

Sheila felt the first stirring of hope. "Yes. I haven't lied to you. You don't have to kill anybody. You and me, together we can break this thing. I do want to help you, Dusty."

"Why?" he asked innocently.

"Because you're my friend." She smiled. "Don't you remember this afternoon, I asked you out?"

"Would you still want to go out with me?"

"After you get help, yes. We can do that."

"What would we do?"

"Go to McDonald's, I don't know."

He smiled dreamily at the thought. "That would be fun." Then his smile faded. "But it won't happen. I still have to kill Dixie."

Sheila was anguished. "But why?"

He coughed, as if there was a layer of dust in his lungs he could not shake free. He pointed the revolver at Dixie's head. When he spoke next, it was in a voice that was scarcely his own, a voice that could even have belonged to a woman, a dead German madame.

"There is no why," he said.

Dixie closed her eyes and screamed.

"Shoot me instead!" Sheila blurted out.

Dusty paused. "No."

"I am more innocent than this tramp," Sheila said. "Didn't you see her in those shorts this afternoon? And her father was right there. Imagine how she dresses when she's out on the town? Imagine how many guys she's slept with already. She's not an innocent. She's a slut, all cops' daughters are sluts. You're wasting your bullets. Kill me, I'm still a blessed virgin."

Dusty stared at her quizzically. "You never slept with Matt?"

"No," she lied.

"But if I let Dixie go, she will tell her father about me. That wouldn't be good."

Sheila spoke passionately. "It won't matter. You'll have your six innocents. You'll be free. The pain will have stopped, Dusty. It will be over.

He went immobile for a moment. Then he nodded. "That's all that matters." He glanced at Dixie with a look of distaste. "Get out of here before I change my mind."

Dixie ran out of the cave.

She didn't even look at Sheila as she left.

Sheila understood. Who wanted to look at a corpse?

Dusty pointed his gun at her. "Is it all right if I bury you here?"

She lowered her head. After all that had transpired, she still could not understand why this was happening. The millions who perished in Auschwitz and Dachau, as the gas had filled the chambers, had probably wondered the same thing. Yet Scheimer and Dusty had answered it all for them, in a way. There was no why. There was just this bitter end.

"I don't give a damn where you bury me," she whispered.

"Goodbye, Sheila. I'm sorry about this."

She heard the click of the revolver hammer being drawn back.

She closed her eyes.

Still, it was not over.

"Sheila!" a voice called from the entrance of the cave.

16

Matthew Jaye was driving Captain Gossick's car. He had driven it all the way from Ventura, and now they were out in the desert—with Mrs. Garcia in the backseat guiding them—and they were lost. What Matt had feared most had turned out to be true. Mrs. Garcia had followed Dusty only partway before Dusty had turned off the road and vanished into the desert. Mrs. Garcia could not remember where that turnoff was. At present they were heading south on 395, retracing their steps, because Mrs. Garcia felt they had gone too far north. Matt kept expecting her to tell him to stop and go back the other way. Sheila was all he could think about. His nerves were raw.

"This is hopeless," Matt said.

"We have to keep looking," Gossick said. "There is nothing else we can do."

"We can't keep looking because we don't know

what we're looking for," Matt complained. He jerked a thumb over his shoulder. "Only she can look, and I think she's going to sleep."

Gossick shook his head. "Mrs. Garcia is doing everything she can to help us." He pointed up ahead. "Why don't we stop at the top of this rise and get out and look around. We'll have a bit of a view from there. I have binoculars in my trunk."

"You have flare guns and binoculars back there," Matt said, feeling like he was losing it. "Do you have a Geiger counter? Do you have an inflatable raft? Do you have a grenade launcher?"

Gossick gave him a worried glance. "I do have the raft."

Matt chuckled bitterly. "I hope it rains then."

They reached the top of the rise and pulled over to the side of the road and parked. They were not up that high, just enough to see over the many ups and downs of the highway. Plowing the road at high speed had been like riding a roller coaster. Gossick got out his binoculars and scanned in every direction.

"What are we looking for?" Matt complained.

"Anything suspicious," Gossick replied.

"Yeah, right," Matt muttered, like they could wait another five years for that.

Yet they saw something interesting not five minutes later.

A car traveling north on 395 at high speed suddenly slowed and turned east off the highway into the dust and sand. Gossick pointed it out and quickly handed the binoculars to Matt. More intriguing was the car that came two minutes after it, which did the exact same thing except it turned off its lights the moment it went off the main highway. Matt thought the cars were about two miles distant, but Gossick said distances were deceptive in the desert. They were probably closer to seven miles away, the old man said.

They looked at each other for a moment as Matt lowered the glasses.

"Are you thinking what I'm thinking?" Matt asked.

Gossick nodded. "Dusty grabbed Dixie and didn't know he had Sheila on his tail."

Matt turned toward the car. "Let's get that bastard before she tries to get to him."

"This is like fifty years ago," Gossick agreed, and there was a note of excitement in his voice.

Yet they missed the turnoff point the first time they passed it. The dust had settled by the time they arrived in the vicinity, and even with the moon it was hard spotting a couple of tire tracks. They had to retrace their steps slowly, the passing seconds especially hard on Matt. Finally, though, they believed they had the right dirt road. Matt turned off the highway and roared forward. Gossick cautioned him to slow down.

"You saw me watching them through the binoculars as we drove down here," Gossick said. "They made another right-hand turn. We can't overshoot that turnoff."

"We have to get to Sheila," Matt swore, slowing reluctantly.

"We'll get to her in time." Gossick patted Matt's leg. "That's a promise."

Matt forced a smile. "The promise of a Jedi?"

"If you like. We're almost there, I can feel it."

A Joshua tree, its withered arm bent toward the south, alerted them to the next turnoff. Matt had killed his lights by this time, driving by the light of the moon. They had not gone far on this last trail when he spotted Sheila's car up ahead. He pulled up beside it.

She was not inside.

"Should we park here and walk?" Matt asked Gossick.

"No. Sheila parked here only because she was trying to sneak up on Dusty. But Dusty must have parked farther in front of us. They've both got fifteen minutes on us. Keep going until we see his car."

They found it only a quarter of a mile away—a red Ford escort, the suspicious small car Lt. Black had told them about. It, too, was empty. Gossick checked inside with a flashlight for signs of blood. There were none. But there were clearly visible tracks in the sand. Gossick got his flares out of the trunk. He spoke to Mrs. Garcia, who continued to sit in the backseat of his car.

"You will be safe here until we return," he said. "We will take care of Dusty."

She squeezed his hand. "Thank you, sir. Dusty—he no good."

"Ain't that the truth," Matt said.

They started across the moonlit desert.

An old man and a boy.

But they didn't feel that way.

They were warriors in a holy battle against evil.

Even Matt, cynic that he was, felt something special wash over him as he walked through the night. But he could not have said what it was or even be sure he wasn't imagining it.

"It's like a mantle," Gossick said out of nowhere.

Matt was intrigued. "So you can read minds, too?"

Gossick took in a deep breath of the night air. "No. But I can read the signs."

They came to the cave minutes later. A hole into shadows. Yes, shadows because there were flickers of light inside, voices and heavy breathing. They were about to enter when a frightened young girl almost ran them over. Gossick grabbed her as she flew by. He had lost none of his reflexes.

"Dixie?" he asked.

She nodded.

"Is Sheila inside?" Gossick asked.

She nodded.

"Is Dusty inside?" Gossick asked.

She nodded.

"Does he have a gun?" Gossick asked.

She nodded vigorously.

Matt whirled and shouted into the cave. "Sheila?"

"I wanted to take him by surprise," Gossick swore.

"You can hardly do that in a cave this size," Matt said. "At least he knows we're coming. That might be enough to stop him from shooting Sheila. Let's go."

"Run to my car," Gossick told Dixie. "It's parked next to Dusty's. Wait there, we won't be long."

The girl fled. They entered the cave, Gossick first, his flashlight in one hand, his gun in the other. Matt trailed impatiently, stumbling over the old man. They could see another flashlight up ahead, flickering in their direction, stinging their eyes.

"Hurry," Matt implored Gossick.

"We don't want to rush him. He'll just start shooting."

The cave widened at the rear. The place was cool. Mounds of sand hugged the uneven brown walls. Matt knew them to be graves. Dusty stood with Sheila clasped in front of him as a shield, his gun pressed to her right temple.

"I did not shoot the other girl," Dusty said calmly. "But I am going to kill Sheila. Nothing is going to stop me."

Gossick lowered his gun and stepped forward. "We were just at your house, Dusty. We'd like to talk to you about that."

"I do not want to talk about my house. Leave now."

"It's your mom we want to talk about," Gossick said.

The old man knew the buttons to push, Matt saw. Dusty was instantly interested. "What about my mom?" Dusty asked.

"She wasn't doing so well when we found her," Gossick said.

"What was wrong with her?"

"She's dead, Dusty," Gossick said. "Tania's dead."

A spasm shook Dusty. But he did not lose his hold on Sheila. "How do you know her name?" he asked quietly.

"I knew her when she was a child," Gossick said. "I knew her mother as well."

"I told him about his grandmother," Sheila whispered. She was scared, of course, but she was cool, too, Matt could see that. Her hope lay with Gossick. Yet Matt didn't know if the old war veteran would be enough. He had this idea—if he suddenly rushed Dusty, the bastard would have to turn and shoot. In that time he would be vulnerable to Gossick's attack. He was not afraid to sacrifice his life if it meant saving Sheila. He began to move slowly off to the left, closer to the walls of the cave. Dusty did not seem to notice, intent as he was on Gossick.

"She was a bad woman, Dusty," Gossick said. "I

met her in Germany in the war. I met her in Los Angeles after the war."

Dusty nodded. "You're the one who killed her."

Gossick took another step closer. "That's right. And if you shoot Sheila I will kill you. That's the simple truth of it. But I don't want to kill you, Dusty. I cared about your mother. She lived with me for a little while. She was not like your grandmother, she was a good person. If she were here now, she would not want you to hurt Sheila. Think back, Dusty, before your mother lost her mind. Remember how she took care of you, loved you."

Dusty sweated, even in the cold cave, the beads of perspiration began to run over his chalk white face. "I have a bad memory," he said.

"It isn't that bad," Gossick said. "You remember leaving your home tonight, don't you?"

"I don't want to talk anymore," Dusty said wearily, his breathing heavy. "I have to do Sheila, then I can rest."

"What did you do before you left your house?" Gossick insisted.

"I don't want to talk anymore!" Dusty shouted. He whipped his pistol around and pointed it at Matt, who had been about to leap. "Stop! I'll kill you all!"

Matt! Don't!

Sheila, despite her predicament, understood everything that was happening in the cave. Gossick was trying to shock Dusty with the reality of what he had done to his mother, probably with the idea of getting Dusty to drop his guard so that he could shoot him the same way he had shot Scheimer. Matt was clearly thinking about trying to be the big hero, and getting himself killed in the process. But none of these acts, devious or foolhardy, she realized, made sense to Dusty because he was just trying to get to number six and there was no logical rhyme or reason why he had to get there. He simply thought when he did he would be able to rest.

That was the key.

She had never had a gun to her head before.

It was not a pleasant sensation.

"Dusty," she said gently. "Can I tell you one more thing before you kill us?"

"Yes," he said.

"Gossick, Matt," she said. "Let me talk to Dusty a minute more before you do anything rash. All right?"

They nodded. She could see they were not going to give her long to talk. Gossick was slowly raising his gun. Matt was tensing his muscles, preparing to jump. Dusty noticed these things as well. He hugged her closer, his breath on her cheek the smell of sorrow. His life had been miserable from the word *go,* she thought. Surely he must want it to be over.

"You need six, right?" she asked Dusty.

"Yes."

"They have to be innocent, right?"

"Yes."

"But the others, the first five, you didn't want to kill them, did you? The voice made you do it."

"Yes."

"You understand that the voice came from your mother?"

"I think so."

"It did, Dusty. We talked about this already. Scheimer used your mother's voice to make you do these bad things. You were forced to do them."

"Yes."

"You see, then, you aren't responsible for what you did." There were tears in her eyes. She was trying so hard and she didn't think it was going to work. Especially when Dusty spoke next.

"I was responsible, Sheila," he said, his voice momentarily clear. "I am not innocent."

Her hope left her then. That is what she had been driving at. That *he* could be number six. That he could put the gun to his head and pull the trigger and finally have his rest. She wept openly, beaten.

Yet he loosened his hold on her, slightly.

She was able to turn and look into his eyes.

"I have had this idea myself," he said.

"I don't understand," she said, even though she did.

"To be the last one. To put a stop to it."

"But you were afraid?" she asked.

"I was afraid." He glanced around the cave, at the graves, Matt, and Gossick. "I have never had a friend in my life," he said sadly. "Can you imagine what that was like?"

"No," she whispered.

Dusty nodded weakly. "I don't think anyone can. Things happen, bad things, and there is no one to talk to about them. So you just keep them inside and try to pretend that they didn't really happen. Then after a while there is so much inside that isn't real, and then you don't know what is . . . what is." His voice faltered, his face pinched with pain. "I wish there had been one person to talk to."

"I wish I could have been that person," she said, and she meant it.

His green eyes shone with a film of tears. Yet the film seemed to wash away something covered, denied, a pain too horrible to acknowledge.

"Sometimes you listened to me," Dusty said.

Sheila swallowed. "I tried . . . sometimes."

Dusty nodded. "Sometimes . . . not enough times." Then he shook his head. "But you were my friend. I believed that when we were together in class." He blinked and asked seriously, "Should I believe that now, Sheila?"

Dusty still had her positioned as his shield, but now the feel of his arm around her changed. He was not using her, he was just holding her. Out of the corner of her eye, she saw Gossick move to shoot, Matt to jump. Again she shook her head minutely. They gave her another few seconds. But now Dusty paid them no heed. He was watching her. She could only tell him the truth.

"I don't know, Dusty," she said.

A faint smile touched the corner of his mouth. "Should I do it?"

"No."

"You wanted me to do it a few seconds ago."

"Because I was scared, too. I'm still scared. But I don't want you to shoot yourself."

He nodded, losing his smile, but suddenly somehow more at ease. "I can believe you. You are my friend. I wasn't sure of that until now. Thank you, Sheila." He let go of her. "I should have been number one. Not number six."

"Dusty!" she screamed.

He pushed her aside and pressed his gun to his head.

She fell to the ground. Closed her eyes.

There was a shot. Just one.

A fine spray settled over her head. It must have been his blood, she realized, his brains. Yet it was not sticky or wet, but dry, like dust that had lain undisturbed in a place forgotten by love. She touched the spray with her hands and felt it merge with her tears and become wet again and wash away. Yet there was too much to forget. She sat crying on the ground. She didn't look up.

Even when Matt and Gossick helped her to her feet.

Even as she let them carry her out of the cave.

She felt no joy that it was over.

Because . . .

Epilogue

"Is it over?" she asked Matt as they drove back to the city in her car. They were alone. Dixie was with Gossick and Lt. Black. Gossick had fired off a flare after they had left the cave and Dixie's father had been there in minutes. In all the excitement, Gossick said, he had forgotten about the blasted things. Lt. Black had wept when he saw his daughter. All's well that ends well, Sheila thought. But was it over?

"You mean us?" Matt asked. She was letting him drive.

She sighed. "If there even is an us."

Matt looked at her. "I almost lost you tonight."

"It was close," she agreed.

"I don't want to do that again."

She bit her lower lip. "Do you mean it?"

He reached over and brushed her hair from her

eyes. "There will always be an us, Sheila," he said. "I want you back."

Not all tears were painful. She squeezed his hand.

"I never left," she said.

About the Author

CHRISTOPHER PIKE was born in Brooklyn, New York, but grew up in Los Angeles, where he lives to this day. Prior to becoming a writer, he worked in a factory, painted houses, and programmed computers. His hobbies include astronomy, meditating, running, playing with his nieces and nephews, and making sure his books are prominently displayed in local bookstores. He is the author of *Last Act, Spellbound, Gimme a Kiss, Remember Me, Scavenger Hunt, Final Friends* 1, 2, and 3, *Fall into Darkness, See You Later, Witch, Die Softly, Bury Me Deep, Whisper of Death, Chain Letter 2: The Ancient Evil, Master of Murder, Monster, Road to Nowhere, The Eternal Enemy, The Immortal,* and *The Wicked Heart,* all available from Archway Paperbacks. *Slumber Party, Weekend, Chain Letter,* and *Sati*—an adult novel about a very unusual lady—are also by Mr. Pike.